RUNDOR'S APPRENTICE

For Stacy

Enjoy the adventure!

RUNDOR'S APPRENTICE

CHAD BALK

ChB

4/13/2012

Printed in the United States of America
First Edition: November 2011

10 9 8 7 6 5 4 3 2 1

Summary: Caladur Vandel, a young elf, is thrown out onto the streets and abandoned. He now must relearn everything he has ever thought to be true. The elf struggles with the fact that he has been a menace to society, a realization he can only come to when he is forced to reside with those he tormented. Now, on his own, he tries to make his own way to fame and fortune within the large city of Fatiil. The arena waits for the confused elf to find his path in life.

ISBN 978-1-463-52552-1

1. Fantasy---Fiction. 2. Elves---Fiction. 3. Adolescent Literature---Fiction.

I would like to dedicate this book to my family and friends who were encouraging and kept me going while I wrote this novel.

-1-

"I couldn't believe it. He just expected me to give him a few copper pieces. Just because he was able to hold a tin cup out in front of himself," Caladur Vandel laughed as he stood next to his best friend, Oranton Elennae. The two boys joked around with one another as they found themselves in the midst of a mass of elves.

"Do you really think he would know what do with *our* money?" Oranton replied. "He'd just go waste it on some Ithexar."

"He couldn't afford Ithexar. He would have to buy cheap wine to drown his miserable life," Caladur corrected.

The two elves, both in their late eighties, were considered young amongst their own. Each was still about thirty years away from reaching "adulthood" within the Order. Both young men were waiting for the Royal Order of True Elves meeting to begin. The ROTE held meetings three times each week for the elven members and no one else.

Within the city of Fatiil, there were many exclusive societies. Although it was difficult to make your way into membership of these groups, it was all but impossible to join the ROTE. In fact, the only way to obtain membership is by proving that you have descended from a line of pure-blood elves. Although this might sound like an easy task, it proved to be impossibly difficult. Not only in Fatiil, but throughout all of Rostanlow, true elves have become an endangered species. The integration of the races was so complete that over the years, line after line of elves allowed their blood to be tainted with the blood of a human, or even a gnome.

The two friends continued their laughter at the expense of the beggars they encountered on their way to the ROTE meeting until Aerandan Talvir, the standing leader of the Royal Order of True Elves, called the session to Order.

Aerandan stood in front of the members of his society. There were one-hundred-seventy-four elves ending their conversations as they gave their attention to their leader. "Welcome one and all to the Fatiilian chapter of the Royal Order of True Elves. I would like to begin by introducing a few visitors from other chapters across Rostanlow. Today we have a family of four from Cantole. They came to Fatiil to visit with their family, the Niialo's."

A family of four elves stood up from their seats in the hall. Caladur stood and applauded for the visiting family, as was customary, with the rest of his fellow pure blood elves. After a brief moment of recognition, the Niialo's took their seats once more and Aerandan resumed his monologue.

After the updates, words of encouragement to stay pure and a telling of the history, the meeting turned to the declaration of elven superiority. The code they each learned early on in their lives. Something they heard over and over in their homes and three times each week at the Royal Order of True Elves. It was a simple code, once you knew it, but as a child it proved difficult to learn. The entire congregation of elves began to recite the code together. "We, the elves of the Royal Order of True Elves, are the superior race. We commit to the Order our lives. We commit to the Order our resources. We commit to the Order our relations. We vow to never taint our blood with that of non-elves. We vow to never withhold business from fellow members. We vow to always stay true to the Royal Order of True Elves. Nothing can tear us apart as long as we stay united."

The meeting of the ROTE was adjourned and the mass of elves began making their way out of the Order's meeting hall into the entrance hall.

The meeting hall itself was magnificent. High, vaulted ceilings with beautiful tapestries of every color of the rainbow draped gracefully from the ceiling to the walls. Light filtered through the tapestries giving the room an almost unreal, regal feeling. The chairs were, in the opinion of Caladur, the most comfortable in the city. Aerandan's podium was well crafted, like only an elf could manage. The emblem of the Order was carved flawlessly into the face of the sturdy wood; a large, healthy oak tree with branches full of luscious leaves and a bright sun peeking out from behind the tree on all sides with rays of light emitting from the center. That symbol brought with it pride, meaning, and life. In addition to the décor and the podium, the room was perfect. It was situated in a circular design with ideal acoustics.

Throughout the city, there were a few other buildings that the Order owned, but the meeting hall was the most important. The entrance hall was just as elegant as the meeting hall. Again, tall ceilings were supported by the walls. High on the walls, well-crafted windows granted bright sunlight access into the hall. The young elf smiled as the sunlight bathed his fair, exposed skin in warmth. The happiness of his life filled him up as he began laughing with his friends as they exited the hall. Without the Order, Caladur had no idea what his life would be like. On rare occasions, his mind would wander in that direction, but he was unable to comprehend it.

"You think the bum is still outside?" Oranton asked as he gave his friend a jab in the ribs.

"If he is, I think I have some fine elven spit for his cup," Caladur jested as he exited the entrance hall to the disgustingly integrated streets of Fatiil.

-2-

The large city sat in the northwestern region of Rostanlow. Fatiil was the entire world for Caladur. He had never been outside of the walls. He never even wanted to be outside of them. Everything he ever could want was within the city. He had good friends, he had a beautiful girlfriend, and he had an entire metropolis worth of experiences ready to be had.

Caladur led his friends through the streets of the bustling city. The Order's hall was located at the far end of the business district of Fatiil. Between their homes and the hall was a slew of hole-in-the-wall stores, none of which they would be caught dead in, the city's arena, and the city's "slum".

A chorus of loud advertisements being shouted by the shopkeepers pierced Caladur's tall, elven ears. He did his best to ignore the shouts but the worthless mixed blood's words managed to penetrate his mind.

"Finest wine in the city!" one man called after the elves.

Oranton stopped to address the winery's employee. "I'll try a glass," he declared as he reached down into his pouch to retrieve a few copper pieces which were handed to the vender.

"I spotted you from a mile away," the street vender decaled, "I thought to myself, 'Now that young man knows what a good wine is when he spots it.'" The vender poured a generous cup of the red wine and handed it to the elf. "Now you take a sip from that and tell me it's not the best you've ever tasted."

Oranton ceased his act as soon as he held the clay wine glass in his left hand. He raised the cup and sucked a mouthful of wine before regurgitating it back out all over the shop keeper. Oranton did not stop there. He threw the fragile, clay piece of drink-ware onto the dirty ground, causing it to shatter into seemingly hundreds of tiny pieces. "Your putrid grape juice cannot compare to the elven wine of the Royal Order of True Elves!"

Caladur and Oranton strolled away from the down hearted human who was preoccupied in an attempt to salvage his cup which was far past the point of repair.

"I can't believe you let that low life's *wine* touch your lips." Caladur said.

"Did you see his face? Completely worth it."

The elves continued on their way past the other shop keeps. For each sales pitch they heard, they had an underhanded remark.

"Eggs for sale. Cheapest in all of Rostanlow."

"And only half are spoiled."

"Finest cloth found here. Tailoring is free."

"Free of skill."

"And style," Caladur added.

"Tools! Get your tools here. They can fix anything and everything."

"Can they fix the broken mallet I bought from him last week?"

"Rum! Ale! Whiskey! Wine! Drink to your heart's content."

"I'd abstain from the bottle the rest of my life before associating with dirty blood."

The shops began growing in both size and prestige as the pair began exiting the market district and entering the arena district.

Caladur hated the arena district. It was full of everyone he despised. The ruthless brutes who fought for a day's wage were unbelievable. The poor peasants who couldn't afford any other type of entertainment plagued the district with their presence. They were on every corner begging for money. Not to eat with, but to gain admission to the arena where they would waste their day away. These rats didn't offer anything productive to the city. Instead, they funneled pity, or stolen, money into a business that simply perpetuated this flawed system. Then, in contrast to these types, the dirty blooded rich folk would bet upon the lives of the arena participants. Caladur wished that he could put money on their fates in a fight to the death. Either way, Fatiil would be plagued with one less dirty man. Of course, this was all speculation. The elf had never actually been inside the arena.

Despite his distaste for the arena, Caladur and Oranton kept their mouths shut as they passed through. Not out of respect, but due to fear. Although they were brutes with tainted blood, they were still brutes. The shop keeps wouldn't respond to the harassment, but the people in the arena district wouldn't think twice before putting either, or both, of the elves into their places.

Rundor's Apprentice

"Come one come all
To the place where men fall
Rundor the Great
Will improve your fate
You've all seen him fight
And always prove his might
From tiger to boar
He's ready for more
An apprentice he seeks
Don't come if you're meek
The greatest he'll choose
All others will lose
Endurance, strength, and dexterity
You must pass these three tests with clarity
If you feel that you can be
Come on over and see
It begins in just two weeks
To all your friends go speak
The one Rundor chooses will win
And then, their training will begin"

Caladur felt nauseous as the scrawny gnome repeated his speech from the top of an old crate. "Who would ever choose to subject themselves to that kind of life?"

"Who cares? We'll never have to worry about that, as long as we have the Order."

The two elves made their way out of the arena district and into the slums. The last scarred part of the city they passed through every time they went to the ROTE meeting.

If the arena district was hell, the slums would be a small corner in the depths where the worst of the worst were imprisoned for eternity. Small buildings, each

identically horrific, stood, if you call it standing, in rows.
The shambled homes gave enough protection to whatever
cockroach of a person happened to crawl inside for the
night. On a normal day, the two elves would go to town on
the maggots residing in the slums, but the streets seemed
to be empty that day.

"Maybe they finally learned their lesson and stayed
inside, waiting for their death," Oranton said while
laughing sarcastically.

"If only we were so lucky," Caladur replied before
pointing further down the street.

A young boy, perhaps ten years old, sat on the
ground. He was leaning against one of the "walls" of a
shack. As the elves approached, they realized the boy was
crying silent tears.

When the boy realized he was no longer alone, he
looked towards the elves with a hopeful smile. "Can you
please," the boy didn't continue his plea. He stared at the
well dressed elves without making another noise as they
strolled right on by. Not a single word, glance, or thought.
The young child reclaimed his spot against the shack and
resumed his weeping.

Caladur and Oranton continued walking out of the
slums and into a wealthy housing district. After dropping
Oranton off at his large house, Caladur made his way back
to his own home. He walked through the superbly
manicured lawn as he approached his residence. The large
house soon enveloped him in shadow. The shade was
welcoming. After the long walk from the Order's meeting
place to his home, he was ready to sit down and rest for a
few hours before going back out.

-3-

Caladur walked with a slight skip in his step towards the home. The private walk was paved with precisely cut stones alternating in color between a deep maroon and a stoic grey. The walk narrowed to a width of six feet and proceeded underneath archways of green shrubs. Aervaiel's home put Caladur's to shame. After emerging from the archway pass, Caladur ascended three round stairs which led to Aervaiel's front door. A golden door knock bearing the mark of the Royal Order of True Elves sat in the center of the heavy door.

Caladur knocked on the door with confidence as he had done almost every day for the past two months. Ever since he began officially dating Aervaiel, his life had been on the up and up. He thought about the girl as he waited for her to come to the door from somewhere within the large home. Not only was her family the wealthiest within the Order, she was, by far, the prettiest elf in Fatiil. At first,

Oranton had been jealous of their relationship. He, like every other young, single elf, had a crush on Aervaiel. Caladur, however, happened to be the one she chose. Oranton had lost his jealousy for the couple about a month ago and now actually seemed to support his friend.

The door opened. Aervaiel's bright smile was contagious. She had been sick for the past few days, but now she was over the virus that ailed her. Caladur lunged forward to give his girl a proper welcome. They shared a long, tight embrace before he briefly kissed her delicious lips and relinquished.

He missed everything about her. The sweet smell of her long, straight, blonde hair, the bright blue eyes that could pierce any soul, the warmth of her perfect body being held against his own, the butterflies he felt every time their lips met in blissful congress, and the way her clothes fit her in a way most men could only see in their dreams.

"You seem to be feeling better," Caladur observed with a grin across his face.

"I am," she replied with a heavenly sigh before hugging her boyfriend again. "I can't wait to get out of this place. I've not been out for days. What's the plan?"

"I thought we could head over to the Royal Brew for a while. People have been concerned for you."

"Perfect. Let's go," she pulled her door closed. The couple held hands as they strolled back down the walk towards the Royal Pub & Brewery.

The Royal Pub & Brewery was, in Caladur's opinion, by far the finest business establishment in the city. It was nothing like the other pubs in Fatiil. The liquor that was served was of the highest quality. The food was superb. The music was glorious. The décor was, for lack of a better word, perfect.

By the time the couple arrived, the sun had set. That was one of Caladur's favorite parts of being an elf. He didn't really need to sleep. Every night, for only a few hours, he would go into a trance-like state. He was still somewhat functional. He, like most elves, used his trance time to read. Since he only needed a few hours of trance, he had the rest of the night to live it up.

After being admitted to the Royal Pub, they took seats across from each other at an open booth in the fairly empty pub. The couple began catching up with each other while they waited for someone to take their order. The booth had enough seats for four people. They assumed Oranton would occupy one after a short while, the fourth normally remained vacant. Being members of such an exclusive club and refusing to associate with others led to a small, tight group of friends and acquaintances.

"I'll just take a burger. I think she wants a salmon filet."

"Thanks. It'll be up in a few minutes," the elven waitress retreated to the kitchen to prepare the food for the couple.

"Thank you," Aervaiel said sweetly as she grabbed Caladur's hand and gently squeezed.

"So how is everything? Did your dad's deal go through?"

"Yeah. He got the entire company. Now, in addition to his other businesses, he is the owner of the North-Western Trade Company. By far his largest asset."

"That's great!" Caladur smiled.

"Yeah. He said he's going to be putting an extension on our home to celebrate the new acquisition. But that's just a start. He mentioned the possibly donating a sum to the Order so that the True Elves Inn can be expanded as well."

The food was delivered a short while later. The burger was delicious. The Royal Pub only served the best cuts of beef. It was fantastic. Aervaiel seemed to enjoy the fresh salmon served with a fruit salad.

"Are you going to spar tonight?" Aervaiel asked between bites.

Caladur finished chewing and swallowing a bite of his burger. "I was hoping to. I beat Oranton the other day and he wants a rematch."

"He never does take a loss well."

"He was fine yesterday at the Order. I walked home with him. Same old thing. He gets pissed and then forgets about it after a day or so. Same thing happened when we started dating."

"So you're going to fight him again?"

"Yeah. And I'll probably beat him again. He'll realize I'm,"

"Hey guys!" Oranton called as he took a seat on the bench next to Aervaiel. "Had dinner without me again? Thought you would, so I already grabbed a bite before I came. Good to see you out of bed Aervaiel. Looks like you're feeling better." He spread his arms out on the back of the bench. Aervaiel didn't notice, but Caladur felt a spark of jealousy when he saw his friend put his arm around, or behind, but close enough, his girlfriend. "So we still on for tonight? Give me a chance to put you back into your place? Caladur?" Oranton snapped his fingers a couple times in front of Caladur's face.

"Uh. Yeah. I'll let you try, but I'd be putting my money on me. I think I'll take you again." Caladur forced his mind to get past his friends "move" and reached for Aervaiel's hand. "A new season's coming, and I'm ready for anything you send my way."

"Good to hear, because it's coming," Oranton sounded as if he was hinting at something, "Now, let's get some drinks. Oranton ordered two elven wines, one for each of the boys, and a glass of white wine for Aervaiel. The friends caught up for an hour as they sipped on their drinks. The pub began to fill with the elves of the Order. No one else was allowed inside the Royal Pub. Every now and then, a traveler would try to enter for a drink, but the barkeep gives a strong hint that they're not welcome. Some people call the *small hint* severe, others call it a sword. If the intruder refuses to leave, well, the Order does everything it needs to do in order to keep the image pure. Although it rarely occurred, nothing was worse than cleaning the spilt dirty blood of the men who refused to leave and ignored the threats.

After the middle of the night came and went, the three made their way out of the Royal Pub and towards the TER, True Elf Rings.

Like the pub, the Rings were on the Southern side of Fatiil. The streets were empty for the most part. The guard, most were at least half bloods, patrolled the dark streets. The drunks were already in the slums, sleeping off their liquor. The late nights held some of Caladur's favorite times in the city. It was peaceful, and the streets were clear of most of those plagued with the misfortune of not being born an elf.

After the short walk in the cool night air, the three elves arrived at the True Elf Rings. Caladur led the way into the building. Like everything else overseen by the Royal Order of True Elves, the TER was ornately decorated, properly situated, and perfectly clean.

The sounds of battle could be heard echoing throughout the large complex. Sticks of wood clapping against each other as attacks were blocked.

Quarterstaff sparring had become a popular pastime for the elves of the Order. Caladur and Oranton had been practicing their quarterstaff skills for well over forty years each. Oranton had, up until recently, always had the edge over Caladur. In the past couple weeks, however, Caladur spent more time than ever at the TER practicing his skills. Now, he was not only comparable with Oranton, but seemed to be genuinely better.

The three friends approached the ledge and looked down upon the sparring rings. About twenty feet below them sat eight different circular rings. Each ring had a diameter of fifteen feet and was elevated an inch above the rest of the floor. Two lines, each two feet long, sat opposite each other within each circle, ten feet apart. Five of the rings were currently in use by other members of the ROTE. Although this compound was open to the public during daytime hours, it became exclusive for members of the ROTE after sundown all the way to sunup.

After watching the sparring for a few minutes, Caladur and Oranton made their way into the pits while they left Aervaiel on the observation deck with the other women at the True Elf Rings. The boys first made their way into the changing room to don the traditional sparring uniforms. Caladur was white while Oranton put on his black uniform. The two man sport has been light verses dark since it began hundreds of years ago. The uniforms were tailored specifically for elves. The cloth was hung with elegance from both of their thin frames. Their fine blonde hair flowed like a peaceful stream down the backs of the traditionally colored tunics.

Once both of the combatants were ready, they retrieved an elven quarterstaff and made their way to an open ring. Caladur approached the white line while Oranton stood ten feet away on the black line. The two men began reciting the traditional chant for their color before the battles began.

"For the power of light I will fight."

"The darkness hour has brought me power."

The two men bowed to one another and the first bout began.

Oranton was the first to make a move. He lunged forward while swinging his quarterstaff at Caladur's nimble feet. Caladur firmly planted his weapon on the floor blocking the attempted sweep and created a foundation to support his weight as he jumped up to kick Oranton squarely in the chest. He rolled backwards, absorbing most of the blow, but found himself near the edge of the platform. He refocused to find Caladur charging towards him to deliver the final blow. Oranton poised himself for his friend's powerful swing. After the blow, his left arm found the floor, an inch below the ring. He had lost.

Caladur helped Oranton back onto the ring and to his feet. After shaking off the previous bout, the two men recited the appropriate slogan and bowed. Their sport was set up to be fought in multiple bouts. If one elf touches the ground outside of the ring, the other elf scores a point. The first elf to accumulate three points wins the competition.

In the second bout, Oranton again began the assault. Instead of performing a risky sweep like last time, he held the quarterstaff firmly in both hands. He shuffled towards his opponent with his weapon at the ready. Once he was close enough, he shoved his staff forward in an attempt to knock his adversary towards the edge of the ring. Oranton moved quickly. Another shove then he began an assault of uppercuts with either end of his polearm. Right, left, right, right, left, shove, left, right. For every attack, Caladur had an answer. Although no hits were landing on Caladur's flesh, Oranton continued his assault as he steadily worked his enemy towards the edge of the ring. With his opponent inches from the edge, Oranton's assault became wild with speed. Left, left, left, left, left, left, left, right. The final right was backed by all of Oranton's strength. A split second later, he was once again on the floor outside of the ring. When he attempted his final blow, Caladur rolled the opposite way, allowing Oranton to tumble out of the ring from his own forceful attack.

Two to zero. Caladur.

Oranton ignored Caladur's hand as he pulled himself back to his feet and re-entered the ring. Although no words were shared, Caladur could clearly see that Oranton was losing his temper. The two elves recited the traditional text and bowed. Before resuming an erect posture, Oranton lunged himself at Caladur. The dark elf dropped his quarterstaff and succeeded in tackling Caladur to the ring's floor. Caladur was pinned under his opponent's furious body. Caladur absorbed several knees, kicks, and punches as he struggled to escape this unprecedented, and illegal, onslaught. The rules, and traditions, of the sport forbade any type of fist combat. Blows could be delivered through one's knees, feet, and quarterstaff, nothing more.

Although Oranton ignored the rules, Caladur managed to get out from underneath. He got on top of his fellow elf, grab his quarterstaff, and begin his own relentless assault. However, his attacks were legal. His temper had left. If there was one thing he despised more than dirty blood, it was cheaters. Rules and laws were set for a reason, and the reason was not so they could be broken. These thoughts flooded his head as he relentlessly attacked Oranton's now bloody head with his quarterstaff. Finally, he stopped moving.

A knockout was an instant win, even if it occurred in the first bout. Caladur stood up to find an elderly elf standing by the side of the ring. "I think that's enough for you both tonight. I'll see to him, you head on home now." Caladur respected his elder and made his way back to the changing room. He returned his quarterstaff and uniform to their proper places before ascending to the observation deck. Aervaiel was waiting for him. To his surprise, she didn't appear to be pleased with his success.

"Did you need to knock him out?" she asked while giving him a perturbed stare.

Caladur was speechless.

"He's not going to let you live this down."

"He will. He always does."

"At any rate, you should get home. I'll wait for him and try to calm him down so he doesn't do anything stupid."

"C'mon. He'll be fine. Walk with me," Caladur urged.

"Na. It's for the best. Good job tonight. Now go get some rest." Aervaiel kissed Caladur before he retreated out of the True Elf Rings.

-4-

Caladur sat between his mother, Eruriel, and Aervaiel. The meeting for the Royal Order of True Elves was coming to a close. Aerandan held his place at the podium looking over the elves in attendance. "We do have one last bit of business to tend to. As many of you know, Eruriel Vandel has been raising her son, Caladur Vandel, for the past nine decades. Her mate fell to the temptations of tainted blood and left the two alone. Since then, her wealth has been dwindling. As a woman, she has no hopes of obtaining employment of means. Her family is in need or else they will be forced to give up their home."

This was all news to Caladur. He knew his mother had been talking about money more frequently than normal, but he did not know it was this serious.

"As you all know, we, the Royal Order of True Elves, help those of us in need. We have amassed a monetary gift for the Vandel family. It should prove to be an adequate amount to buy enough time for Eruriel to find a suitable elf to match with. Please, if you find it in your heart, consider giving the family anything you can. If you would like a gift to be anonymous, please come see me after the meeting. Thank you for your help, I know I can speak on behalf of the Vandel's who certainly thank you in their time of need. Now, I would like to call this meeting of the Royal Order of True Elves to a close.

The mass of elves stood up and recited their code. "We the elves of the Royal Order of True Elves are the superior race. We commit to the Order our lives. We commit to the Order our resources. We commit to the Order our relations. We vow to never taint our blood with that of non-elves. We vow to never withhold business from fellow members. We vow to always stay true to the Royal Order of True Elves. Nothing can tear us apart as long as we stay united."

Caladur had not been more embarrassed at any point in his life. Had he known anything about the struggles his mother was going through, had he known anything about being called out in front of the entire Order, he would have asked Aerandan to use a little more discretion. Caladur caught a glimpse from Aervaiel as she quickly made her way out of the Order's hall. Not even a word of goodbye from his girlfriend. Oranton snickered as he walked by. At least that was something. He hadn't heard a word from him since he beat him at the Rings. Oranton's face was still cut and bruised from the vicious assault of Caladur.

The ashamed elf was forced to wait with his mother while the rest of the members filed out of the hall he normally looked forward to being in. Now, all he wanted was to be gone. After most of the crowed had left, Aerandan approached Caladur and his mother.

"I trust you will continue your search for a proper man to support you. As much as I'd like to, the Order cannot support you forever."

"Yes thank you. It's more than generous what you have already done for us. We are completely appreciative. Right?"

The way his mother said, "Right" almost made Caladur squirm. It must have been completely obvious to Aerandan that he was not happy to be called out in front of the Order, if his face hadn't already given it away. He mustered up his courage and his most grateful voice to say, "Thanks."

"Not a problem my boy. You be sure to keep your mother safe now. I've heard that you have become quite the warrior." The disappointment seemed to ooze forth from his words. Although Caladur had been well within the legal guidelines of the sport, his loss of temper was not within the confines of being a gentleman, or a proper elf. "Now you two go on ahead and get home."

Caladur walked with his mother back to their home. The manicured lawn hadn't been kept for almost two weeks now and was losing its look. Caladur hadn't noticed the tall grass or unkempt shrubs until that day. He hadn't even realized that the inside of his home was filling with dust until that day.

"Why didn't you tell me?" He asked his mother. A slight whine emitted from his words.

"It's not your problem. It's mine. I'm taking care of it. In fact, it's been taken care of. I've found a buyer for the home. We're moving out next week."

The words hit him like a boulder dropped from the top of a cliff. "Moving? Where?"

"I don't know yet. But we'll figure something out. You can probably stay with Oranton while I find a place."

Caladur's face betrayed him.

"You're not talking again?" His mother guessed, disgusted.

He shook his head.

"Well, I guess you'll need to find somewhere. You have two days. Now go get your things packed as best you can."

His mother had changed over the past ten years. She never used to be so cold. So, uncaring. But something had changed, and Caladur had to live with it. With the knowledge of the monetary crisis, he had something to blame. The elf without anything left to him in the world climbed the stairs in his soon to be ex-home to begin packing the few belongings he had.

As he packed up his room, thoughts of his ex-girlfriend, his ex-best friend, and his ex-home began to flood his already filled mind. He consoled himself with the thoughts that nothing else could go wrong. After all, he still had the honor of being a full blood elf, and the prestige of being a member of the Royal Order of True Elves.

-5-

Caladur hadn't seen any of his friends for the past couple days. He couldn't bring himself to attend the ROTE meeting. The looks, the comments, the rumors, it would be too much for him to take. The buyers of the home were moving in the next day, and Caladur had all of his belongings moved to storage along with his mother's furnishings. Aside from moving their belongings from their home to storage, he hadn't spent time with his mother since she broke the news.

It hadn't been uncommon for her to go into the city to do her own thing on a daily basis, however, over the past couple days, it was more frequent. The adolescent elf only saw his mother once, maybe twice a day.

As the sun began to set on his last day living in his home, he couldn't bear it. He left his home and began walking through the large city without a cause. The bustle

of the city's life did not disgust Caladur in the usual way.
Something about the lifestyle of those not involved with the
Royal Order of True Elves almost intrigued, no, fascinated,
Caladur. He allowed his mind to wander freely as walked
without a thought of his path. Without even thinking about
it, he actually passed up a beggar in the slums without
making any sort of snide remark.

After allowing his mind to wander for close to an
hour, he found himself in the arena district. As he became
aware of his location, he heard a bard recruiting warriors
for the arena once more.

"...to boar
He's ready for more
An apprentice he seeks
Don't come if you're meek
The greatest he'll choose
All others will lose
Endurance, strength, and dexterity
You must pass these..."

Caladur quickly made his way back out of the arena
district. Away from the mixed bloods, the beggars and the
rich men placing bets on the scum who risked their lives
for a few pieces of gold. He did not realize where he was
heading until he found himself standing in front of the
Royal Pub & Brewery.

The young elf stood in front of the establishment for
close to three minutes before he finally made his way
towards the building. His mind was blank except for fear.
He was afraid that he would not be accepted by his friends.
He was afraid that he was making a bigger deal out of the
situation than was necessary. However, he was not afraid

of the horrible event that awaited him as he approached the building.

"I'm sorry sir. But you're no longer welcome here," an elf that Caladur had seen almost every day since he was a young child said. A tone of disgust dripped off of his words as he stood in front of the door, blocking Caladur from entering.

"Excuse me?" Caladur had been blindsided. It didn't seem right. The Order would not ban him from their facilities just because his family was poor. "This doesn't make any sense."

The man said again, with a powerful force this time, "You're no longer welcome here."

Caladur stood his ground. Confused.

"I am going to ask you one more time. Get your dirty blood out of the way or we are going to have a problem here."

Dirty blood? Caladur forced a laugh. His blood was as pure as a winter's first snow. "Alright, jokes over. Let me in."

The bouncer's fist met Caladur's surprised face. Caladur's nose was bleeding onto the ground outside of the Royal Pub & Brewery. "Now I got your filthy blood all over our door step. Get back into the dirty city where you belong."

Caladur, beaten and confused, made his way as slow as a beetle from his face to his feet. When he stood up, he saw two faces he recognized. Oranton and Aervaiel were making their way from the streets of Fatiil towards the Order's restaurant. As they drew closer, Caladur watched while Oranton grabbed the girl's hand. She accepted the hand as she stepped by her beaten ex-boyfriend with the

grace only an elf can possess. Oranton let go of her hand
before she was granted access to the pub.

"Hey man," Oranton said while walking towards his
old friend with a smile.

"What's going on?" Caladur smiled, realizing that his
friend was going to help.

"Obviously they finally realized what you really are. A
piece of mixed blood scum." Oranton spit upon Caladur
before pushing him back to the ground. "It all made sense
when we found out what you really were. Get out of here."
Oranton kicked the beaten elf and made his way into the
exclusive restaurant.

Caladur sat on the dirty ground of Fatiil processing
what had just happened. Everything had been taken away
and he didn't know why. He went to the only place he knew
to go. Aerandan Talvir's home. It was in the same
neighborhood as his home. His old home.

On his way, the horrific event played over and over
again. Of all the terrible things that happened to him in the
past thirty minutes, the worst wasn't seeing his girlfriend
hold the hand of his best friend, it wasn't being spit upon
and kicked by his best friend, it wasn't even being denied
access to the pub. The thing that bothered him the most
was being accused of having dirty blood run through the
veins underneath his own skin. He had had friends come
and go throughout his life. Some moved away, some
diverged from the life of a respectable True Elf. However, he
had been tied to the Order since he was born. He knew
nothing else.

Eventually, he arrived at the home of the Order's
leader, Aerandan Talvir. If anyone knew what was
happening, he would. Caladur made his way to the door
and began knocking away. He was well aware that

knocking like a madman was uncouth, however, his world had just been shattered and he had no self restraint. When he finally stopped knocking away on the door, he heard footsteps approach the door before it finally opened.

"What's going on?" Caladur blurted out.

"I assume you've heard the news. And by your appearance and the time," he glanced at his watch, disgusted. "It must have been rather unpleasant for you." All of the usual emotion from Aerandan was gone. "Wait here please." Aerandan closed the door on Caladur for a few moments as he retreated back into his home.

When he returned, he handed a piece of paper to Caladur. Without another word, he closed the door and secured the lock from within.

Caladur took a look at the paper in the dim moonlight. His keen elven eyes were barely able to make out the lettering on the letter.

To whom it may concern:

It has become clear to us, the Royal Order of True Elves, that your status with us has been illegitimate. Effective immediately, you are banned from all functions of the Royal Order of True Elves. Any attempt you make to enter an establishment under the ownership of the Royal Order of True Elves will be met with unfavorable reprisal. If you feel that this order is incorrect in any way, please feel free to attempt to contact Aerandan Talvir. However, especially in your case, it'll do no good. Your blood has been identified as unclean and unless you are able to prove that your father was in fact a pureblood elf, you will not be allowed to attend any more events of the Royal Order of True Elves.

We do wish you the best in your now unfortunate life.

-Aerandan Talvir

Caladur knocked on the door again. Moments later, it opened.

"Were you unable to read the letter?" The disdain was clear in his voice.

"It said come to you if I had any questions. I've got plenty."

A blank stare.

"Why has my blood been labeled unclean?"

No response.

"Why did this happen now?"

...

"Who brought this evidence to you?"

Finally Aerandan responded. "Your mother can answer all of these questions. I don't believe that she's left yet. I would suggest speaking to her before she leaves. Now, there's nothing you can do. Leave my property before I'm forced to get the guard involved." The elf once again closed the door in Caladur's face.

The young elf, or half-elf rather, was lost in his world. He let his head fall as he walked towards his home in hopes to find his mother. Whether or not he found his mother, he knew that everything, his entire life, had fallen into shambles within the past two hours. He had nothing left. Nothing.

-6-

Caladur sat in a trance. Unlike most nights, he was not reading. His mind was too clouded by the events of the evening. His empty room didn't help console the struggles he was dealing with. As the jumble of thoughts ran rampant through his head, he heard someone enter the home. He quickly stood at attention, ready to confront his mother.

"Mother!" There was no love in his voice. He now knew that she had been lying to him his whole life. He wanted answers.

His mother appeared to be in shambles. It was clear to him that she had been crying. He didn't care. Her red face and tear stained blouse didn't receive any consoling from her own son. The young man she had raised in this world. "I'm sorry Caladur. That's all I can say."

"That's all you can say?" He was furious. "How about you explain who my father really was. How about you explain why you chose now to tell the Order that I'm not a pure blood? Or why don't you explain to me why you never told me? Do you realize how much of my life I've spent hating other people like me? My entire life has been a lie. Now I've got nothing. And the only person I can find to blame is you."

"I'm sorry," her son's rant had reignited the flow of tears, "I cannot explain anything else to you. I'm sorry about this." She let the tears flow from her eyes a moment before looking at her son again. "You should know that I'm leaving. I won't be coming back here. I cannot bear to live in the city."

Caladur began to settle down as realized the affect the events had had on his mother. "Where are we going?"

The silent tears continued. "We're going nowhere. I'm sorry," the sobbing erupted, "but you're not coming with me. I need to leave the city alone. It's the only way. Now you be a good boy and figure out how to get your feet underneath yourself. Don't be afraid to go beneath what you thought you were. You'll no longer have everything handed to you. You must make a living for yourself. I know you can do it. But I need to leave. The wagon is waiting for me."

Caladur couldn't take it. After everything, his mother was abandoning him.

She turned around one more time before leaving the home. "You'll be fine. You're such a great person and will be able to overcome this small obstacle."

Caladur wracked his brain trying to think of the "small" obstacle he was facing. By the time he snapped back to reality, his mother had left the home, abandoning him. Although he thought he was alone before, now, he truly was alone. He had no friends, no family, no colleagues, not even any acquaintances.

-7-

Someone entered the home. Caladur snapped out of his trance once more to realize that the bright morning sun was shining through his window into his empty room. He rose to his feet with the speed of a jackrabbit understanding that the intruders must be the new home owners. Then his thoughts came to fall upon the truth, he was the intruder. He was staying in a home that no longer belonged to him.

Caladur made his way down towards the front doors of his old home. As he descended the stairs, he came face to face with the family who was moving the first of their belongings into their new home. The two young children were terrified of the disheveled looking elf descending the stairs in their brand new home. The mother attempted to calm her children while the father tackled Caladur to the floor.

In normal circumstances, Caladur would have been able to fend for himself, however, what little will he had left was stripped from him when he saw that his mother sold the home to a family of humans. From their appearance, there was not a single trace of elven blood in their veins. Yet his mother still sold the home to the miscreants.

"I'm leaving!" Caladur shouted after coming to the truth that he couldn't find a way out of the man's hold.

The man did not relinquish his grasp on the young elf until a member of the Fatiil guard arrived at the home. The guard entered the home, followed by the mother and children. The two young human's were beginning to calm down as their father released the intruder into the custody of the Fatiil guard.

"Let's go," the guard barked at Caladur as he pulled the elf up to his feet and secured his arms behind his back with a pair of sturdy manacles.

The guard led Caladur out of the home and through the streets of Fatiil towards the bastion without a word. He felt like a piece of scum on display for everyone to see. Never had he once expected to be on this end of the law. If the elves ever found themselves in trouble with the law, which rarely occurred, they would simply be able to bribe their way out. But Caladur had nothing, not even a single piece of copper.

He was led through the ritzy part of town. The elf hung his head in an attempt to hide his shame from any onlookers he happened to know. It didn't really matter. Anyone he knew or cared about already saw him as nothing. The glamour of the neighborhood didn't appeal to him anymore. Something had changed. A lot had changed. He was living life on the top of the world a couple days ago, now he belonged in the slums. And that's what they walked through next.

He imagined himself crawling up into one of the shambles of the broken down homes in order to keep protected from the elements. The people that sat in the streets of this part of city actually had faces to Caladur now. They weren't just things, they were people. A woman sat on the edge of street and glared at him as he walked by. The pain was clear in her face. She looked like she was feeling the same pain Caladur felt. He thought to himself that she must have once had something worth living for. Then, for some reason that may or may not have been her fault, it was all stripped away.

The guard led him around the arena district to avoid the mass of people that would be gathered there in the morning. They skirted around the north side of the arena's crowd through a district of middle-class housing. This district was filled by those people who held steady jobs but were not wealthy in any sense of the word. The people were beginning to come out of their homes to begin their day just in time to watch Caladur be led by the guard through their street. Some of the people stared, some ignored him, a few even pointed at him and laughed. Many of those who were laughing at him he recognized as those who he made fun of or abused while he believed the elusive thought that he was a member of the superior race. One person in particular stuck out to him. He didn't know what it was, but he caught a glimpse of a girl as he walked by. She had dark brown hair, something that normally repulsed him, but today, in the morning sunlight, was fantastically beautiful. Her somehow normal appearance was more attractive to him than that of Aervaiel, his ex-girlfriend. Her smile almost made Caladur laugh to himself as he was led by the guard. A small dimple in her chin provided a near perfect accent to her beautifully average, human, look. Then just as quickly as she appeared, she was gone, walking away from Caladur as he continued his march towards his imprisonment.

After the seemingly endless parade of shame, Caladur found himself entering the large bastion of the Fatiil guard. The bastion was the central installment of the Fatiilian government. The monstrous building held the offices of most, if not all, of the city's officials within its sturdy walls. The entrance hall was large, but nowhere near as fancy as the Royal Order of True Elves. The guard ushered Caladur swiftly through the entrance and towards a staircase that led down towards the depths of the bastion.

With each step down, Caladur's expectations of his future fell. The pair met the bottom of the stairs and found themselves in a small room furnished with only a table and torches that lit the dim room. "Take a seat," the guard ordered.

Caladur followed the guard's command and sat on the wooden chair on the side of the room. He thought to try to explain his case but decided that it would only cause more problems for him. The elf thought that if he was able to just go along with the process he would be able to get out of the situation with little or no consequence.

After the guard had written out a formal report of the highlights of the incident, he came back to Caladur. "What were you doing in the home?"

"It was my home until today. My mother sold the house and left the city refusing to take me with her. I'm alone and had nowhere else to go. I was planning to leave before they got there, but I didn't know when they would

arrive and I seemed to lose track of time. I didn't mean to
cause any troubles. I've gone through a lot in the..."

"That's enough," the guard cut his prisoner off in the
middle of his confession. "You obviously know that you
were in the wrong to be in the home, you have been
cooperating with me all the way here and you seem to me
to be a good enough guy. Now, I know how you elves work
so I'm not going to take much time on this one. I'm going to
lock you up until your friends come to get you out."

"But,"

"Now don't go starting a problem for me now or else
this will end quite differently for you," the guard warned.
"Now c'mon. The cells are down this way." The guard led
Caladur through the depths of the bastion until they
reached a hallway which ended in a dead-end. On either
side of this hallway were small cells guarded by sturdy,
iron bars. The guard opened one with a key, removed the
manacles securing Caladur's hands and gently guided the
criminal into the cell before closing the rod iron door,
sealing Caladur inside.

-8-

The prison was dark, as if the whole block was a turtle's head that had been retracted into the depths of its shell. There were only a few other prisoners being held within the cells. Caladur knew this wasn't where the hardened criminals were held, that was somewhere deep in the depths of the bastion. This was a short-term block. The hall of cells was populated most frequently by the drunks, rebellious youth and elves awaiting their kin to come and collect them.

The first day came and went with little consequence. The guard's shift changed and the guard who initially brought Caladur to his new home took over. "Good morning," he called to everyone in the cell block before lowering his voice slightly for his colleague, "Still got two?"

"Still got an elf," the guard who had been on duty all
night exclaimed. "The one you brought in yesterday I
think."

The guard looked at Caladur, "Yeah. He's the one."
His voice was distant now, as if he was deep in thought.
After a moment, his trance was interrupted with a slap on
his back.

"I'm off Kani. Snap out of it and have a good one."
The night guard left the hall of cells and ascended the
stairs to the freedom of the outdoors.

Caladur sat, and waited, then sat some more as the
day drifted by. That evening the guard changed again.
Throughout the day, a number of youth had been caged up
and released after a time. It was beginning to become
routine. Then, the guard came up to his cell.

"You're moving." An oversized key opened the cell
door and the guard escorted the elf to another cell further
down the hall, away from the stairs. "We can't justify
putting you with the killers, but we can hold you for a
while. It's not often that we get to hold an elf for more than
a few hours. But you know that already." He locked the
new cell. "Sit tight."

He did.

An hour later, it became apparent that he was moved
next to the human man who had been in the cell block
since Caladur's first night.

"Whasup witchu?" the man asked. His speech was
unpolished. The words were strung together like a child
first learning the concept that 'LMNOP' is in fact five letters,
not one.

Disgusted by the lack of intelligence, Caladur
ignored the man.

"Whachu dumb boy?"

Caladur turned slightly towards the man. "I would never grace you with a response," disdain filled his voice. "Human."

"Sounds t'me like you jes did." He paused and did his best to imitate the elf's voice, "Sonny," despite his terrible performance, he gave himself a long drawn, wheezy laugh. He clapped a few times and repeated himself, "Sonny."

Caladur turned his back to the man completely. His face shamed. The dumb codger was right. He kept his back towards the man all night and for all of the next day.

By the fourth day of his stay in jail, the only other permanent resident was the man who could barely speak. Every so often, the man tried to speak to Caladur again. The elf ignored the attempts.

The prison food, if one could call it food, was beginning to grow on Caladur. It wasn't the prime cuts of meat he was once accustomed to, but it kept him alive. The 'warm' broth flowed down his throat. The gag reflex that had occurred during the first two days was a thing of the past. Caladur turned the crude, clay bowl sideways to fit it though the bars and set it on the floor. "Done," he called to the post where the guard sat for most of the day and night. But, no one was there. A moment later, the guard reappeared with a colleague and an elf.

Caladur recognized the elf from the Order. They weren't friends, but elves of the Order stuck together. The new prisoner was about one hundred years his senior. Caladur searched his mind for the elf's name. After nothing came to mind he just blurted out, "Hey!"

The elf searched the dim cell block with his keen eyes until they settled on Caladur.

The human prisoner stood up and grabbed the bars separating his area from Caladur's. "Now you cantalk. Whata suprise."

Both elves ignored the man.

The new prisoner locked eyes with Caladur and stared for a moment.

Caladur's dark hopes shot out of the dim prison to the evening sky a few yards above him. Then, they were shattered, as if someone tied a few anvils to the hopes and dropped them back into the cell block.

"You're the dirty blood aren't you? The one who pretended to be a full blood for nearly a century. Right?"

Caladur backed further into his cell.

The man, out of character, frowned a bit. No laugh, just pity. From a human.

"You know," the new prisoner continued, "if it weren't for pieces of garbage like you and your mother tainting our kind, the world would be a better place. Really, it just goes to show what mixed bloods really are. As soon as you leave the Order, you get planted in a cell. I guess it's where your kind belongs.

"Lookoos talkin," the human said. His large grin had returned. "Youranelf too. An y're righere injail too." He laughed. "Annoto be rude. Butchoo look like yoove a bit of that dirty blood in them veins ofyurs."

Caladur laughed silently to himself as the human pointed out the holes in the elf's logic.

The elf scoffed at the man who turned to wink at Caladur.

A few hours later, the elf was picked up. He said a few snide remarks as he exited the cell block. The night came and went as the drunk and the youth began filling the open cells. Morning came and the inmates left. The cycle of Caladur's life.

Later in the evening of the fifth day in prison, after the rush of drunks began, Caladur's cellmate reached his hand through the bars to offer a handshake. "Owsin," he said introducing himself.

Caladur turned just enough to see the man on the far edge of his peripheral.

"C'mon you gotta get overit kid. I'm good people. Jeslike yerself." He wiggled his hand a bit, trying to tempt Caladur to shake it. "C'mon. I won bite. Hard." He laughed again.

Caladur looked the man over once, then again. He slowly got to his feet reached out to shake the man's hand as if he was reaching into a pit filled with snakes.

Once his hand was in reach, Owsin grabbed the elf's hand and gave it a good shake. "Now at wasn so bad wasit?"

Caladur lowered his hand, speechless. It felt like any other handshake he's ever been a part of.

"Now you say ur name." Owsin urged before enhancing his toothy grin.

"Caladur," the elf replied quietly. He didn't realize that he was speaking until his ears heard his voice.

"Glata meecha Cally."

Something inside Caladur turned off. He and Owsin spent much of the rest of the evening talking. Caladur, for the first time, told someone about his excommunication from the elves. Unlike the other nights, Caladur was somewhat happy when he went into a trance that night.

The sixth day in prison finally brought change. Just before the evening shift changed, a young boy, maybe ten years old, came into the cell block.

49

"Dad!" the boy called and ran to Owsin's cell. "We got the money from grandma. She said that I could come get you myself. I got the gold right here." The boy pulled out a pouch full of coins from around his neck he had hidden beneath his shirt.

"Tanks buddy." Owsin said as he hugged his son through the bars. "Member how I tolju bout helpin those oo needit more?"

The boy nodded so fast that his hair seemed to defy gravity for a moment.

"Good. Then what I neeju todo is free ma new frien Cally. He's got noone to elp im out. Bail im out an get im some food witha rest."

The boy was clearly disappointed but obeyed his father.

Caladur felt as though he was standing beside himself, he couldn't believe it. The dumb human who couldn't speak well was buying him out of jail.

"What about you?" Caladur finally managed to say.

"I'll be fine. You needit more an I do." He laughed a bit more. "Get outa here Cally. Best of luck to you. Yer good people boy. Donchoo forget it."

The guard on duty, Kani, was the same that captured Caladur six days prior. Before he processed the money for bail he looked over the elf with a pair of stern eyes which he expected his father may have looked upon him with. "Done breaking into homes?"

The elf did not want to try to explain the technicalities involved in his infringement and simply said, "Yes sir."

"Good. Now let's get you out of this place and back up to the streets. I don't wanna catch you down here again. You hear?"

"Yes sir." Caladur smiled as the guard gave his back a little pat ushering him and Owsin's son towards the exit of the cell block.

-9-

He was finally free and felt the sun warm his elven skin once more. In the prison, he had no way of discerning what time of day it was other than watching the guards change shifts. While he expected to find the morning sun low in the sky, he found late afternoon sun, peeking through the clouds, beginning to set in the western horizon. Without anywhere else to go, he began following the sun, heading west within the city.

The elf had only been out of prison for about five hours. The money for his bail was depleted by the guard, leaving no extra for food as Owsin directed. The boy quickly went his own way after leaving the prison, before Caladur could even thank him.

The sun had set and Caladur had nowhere to go. He sat on the side of the street for a while wondering what to do. His stomach was beginning to rumble in protest urging him to eat something. Yet he had no food or money.

The elf wandered through the streets until he found a somewhat busy pub to enter. The *Clay Pitcher*. He kept his head down as he entered the business and took a seat at the bar. After a moment or two a bar maiden came to take his order.

"A turkey sandwich with a glass of water please." He replied. The elf kept his order simple and inexpensive. He needed to eat but knew he couldn't pay for the food. It seemed, to him at least, to be better to steal a cheap sandwich and a glass of water than a steak and a glass of wine.

The food came a short while later. Caladur kept to himself and made no attempt to interact with any of the honest patrons of the establishment. He quickly ate the food and drank his fill of water before looking for an opportunity to exit. Once all of the pub's servers were busy tending to other customers, Caladur slipped away into the streets of Fatiil.

The elf made a few turns to ensure he was free. Once he believed that he was safe, he sighed, only to realize that a man was walking next to him. Kani, the guard who first took him to prison, a place he quickly understood would be his new home. Just as he was beginning to try to talk his way out of the situation, the guard held up a hand to stop him.

"You seem alright. That's why I paid for your food. That's also why I'm not taking you back. But you need to get off this streak. I know life's tough, but you got to find a way that doesn't include theft." The guard reached into his pocket. "Here, take this and don't let me see you around again. Deal?" The guard offered a hand which held a small pouch filled with coins.

"Deal," Caladur coughed out as he took the guard's pouch from the offering hand.

The guard left Caladur as if nothing had happened. Caladur spent the rest of the night walking through the city. His body wouldn't let himself go find a place in the slums. He couldn't bear to do that. He was, after all, an elf. No matter what the Order said.

The next day, everything seemed different to him. The venders announcing the pricing of their merchandise was now important to Caladur. He wasn't in the position to purchase anything he desired. He wasn't in the position to purchase much of anything. The money Kani had given him would only last him long enough to make it a day. The clothes he wore smelled horribly. He had not changed his ensemble for over a week. Not since he was taken to prison.

Caladur began where he knew he needed to. Food. Without the ability to find food to eat, he would be dead. That was the one beneficial parts of being in prison, he was given food. He continued through the city keeping his eyes open for anything that remotely seemed like an employment opportunity.

Shortly later, the sun began setting and the small shops and stands began closing up business for the day. He stopped wandering, took a deep breath, and began walking towards the slums, his new home, where he would sleep for the night. He was passing through the bustling arena district when something he had heard over and over again caught his ear. The small gnomish bard was still stationed on a crate a good distance away from the entrance shouting out his advertisement.

"Don't come if you're meek
The greatest he'll choose
All others will lose
Endurance, strength, and dexterity
You must pass these three tests with clarity
If you feel that you can be
Come on over and see
The day it starts is tomorrow
Don't miss it and fill with sorrow
The one Rundor chooses will win
And then, their training will begin"

The gnome took a deep breath and began again at
the beginning.

"Come one come all
To the place where men fall
Rundor the Great
Will improve your fate
You've all seen him fight
And always prove his might
From tiger to boar
He's ready for more
An apprentice he seeks
Don't come if you're meek
The greatest he'll choose
All others will lose
Endurance, strength, and dexterity
You must pass these three tests with clarity
If you feel that you can be
Come on over and see
The day it starts is tomorrow
Don't miss it and fill with sorrow

The one Rundor chooses will win
And then, their training will begin"

Caladur stopped moving through the crowd. The gnome continued making his advertisement to every passerby as he began his pronouncement at the beginning. Caladur began examining his abilities, hoping that he met the requirements presented by the gnome. He wasn't meek. He had been able to hold his own at the True Elf Rings for years. He had endurance, he had strength, he certainly had dexterity, and furthermore, he felt that he was fully capable at keeping his mind clear through all of his work. After deciding that he was worthy to at least attempt to fill the position of Rundor's apprentice, he realized what he was thinking. "Work for the arena?" He questioned himself out loud. But as much as he wanted to think of a reason not to at least try, he continually came to the realization that it was all he had.

A drop of water appeared on his shoulder. Then another.

The people in the wide open street began to scatter this way and that as they attempted to make their way to cover as quickly as possible. The rain accelerated to a downpour as if the top of the salt shaker had fallen off, unleashing an onslaught of the mineral onto food. Thunder resonated throughout the city. While the people scattered and the gnome ceased his call to employment, Caladur stood motionless, letting the rain wash his dirty body. The elf smiled. He felt free. He was free. He no longer had to concern himself with the traditions, the exclusiveness, or the rude behavior of the elves. He was alone, broke, dirty, and homeless, but he was free.

After the cool, late summer rain had been soaked into his clothes and his skin, he began strolling towards the slums where he was destined to stay for the night. For the first time in over a week, the elf smiled as he walked through the largely vacant streets of Fatiil.

The slums were packed with drunks, junkies, and the homeless. Caladur went from home to home trying to find an empty shelter where he would be able to stay. Door after door he quickly came to realize that the shelters in the slums were not first come first serve, but they were allocated to people. Within the slums he found that there were three different sub-districts. Immediately adjacent to the arena district was the junkie district. Caladur felt discomfort surge through his body as he passed through this section. He didn't have anyone with him and felt that danger surrounded him. Ithexar was the drug of choice for the residents and they would do whatever it took to obtain more. The next sub-section of the slums was reined over by the drunks. Those men and woman who chose to abandon their work, their homes and even sometimes their families for the bottle. This section was not nearly as desolate as the first. The people were harmless for the most part, most were simply eccentric. The elf would have not been happy to stay in this part, but if the option presented itself, he realized that he couldn't turn it down. Finally, on the far end of the slums was a section for families. Mothers accompanied by their small children populated this area of the slums. The division of the slums made sense to him. The mothers wanted to protect their children as best they could, so they took the shacks that were as far as possible from the junkies. The junkies only cared about making just enough money for their next fix, so they took the homes

nearest the arena and business district where they would make the most money begging.

Caladur found himself able to associate with the people in family area the best. They were most like him, victims of unfortunate circumstances. He was mustering up the courage to approach one of the homes to ask for shelter before he came to find one shack that was unoccupied. He hesitantly approached the shambles of a shelter and knocked on the side home. "Hello?" he called to the darkness.

No response.

He made his way into the dark shack. There was no door, just an entryway. Inside he found one simple room. There was nothing to the shack except for four walls and a somewhat stable roof. Rain streamed into the home from small holes in the roof and contributed to the forming puddles on the floor. He spotted one corner full of trash. Everything from spoiled food scraps to small bits of clothes so worn that they were no longer useable in anyway.

Caladur didn't have the luxury of choice. It was this or nothing. He took it. The elf found a dry spot on the floor away from the putrid smelling garbage and took a seat. He entered into his trance. Caladur knew that he needed all the rest possible if he was going to have a chance to secure his position at the arena. The young man cleared his mind of all of his prejudices, preparing to associate himself with all of the different types of people he would encounter as he set forth on his journey to join the arena.

The night was beginning to improve for Caladur, he had a place to stay and he had a somewhat realistic goal for employment. Things were looking up. Then someone entered the home. A mother accompanied by a son and a daughter.

"I'm sorry. I'll be on my way." Caladur said as he stood up and began heading towards the only door of the shack. Memories of being arrested flooded his mind. Then he took a look at the boy. It was the same boy he and Oranton completely ignored just over a week ago. The poor boy had been asking for money so he could buy some food. He had no other way of surviving. All Caladur did was walk right by.

"Wait," the boy said, standing in front of the door, not letting Caladur leave. "I know you."

Caladur froze. The boy remembered the elf that wouldn't give a starving boy a short moment of his life. The elf began to summon the courage to apologize, but the boy spoke again first.

"Mom, can he stay with us tonight? He needs a place." The boy's voice was earnest.

His mother returned a stern look at her son before sizing Caladur up. "Why are you here? Spend too much money on the Ithexar? Or was it the booze?"

"No neither. My mother abandoned me. I've got nothing else. I just need one night. Then I'll be out of your hair. Please ma'am." Caladur never once thought he would find himself pleading to a homeless human.

After a moment that held Caladur's safety in suspense, the mother agreed. "Just one night. And so help me. If you try anything, I'll not think twice about cutting your throat in front of my little ones." The woman revealed a crude dagger from her pocket. She never cared for violence, but living on the streets sometimes required a few tough words accompanied by the will, and ability, to follow through.

"You don't need to worry. My name is Caladur. Thank you. What should I call you?"

"My name is Estine. This is my daughter Celeste, and my son Lucas. Please Caladur, do not make me regret this. I'd hate to have to do something rash in front of the eyes of my children." Estine changed her demeanor in an instant and shifted into mother mode. "Alright you two, it's getting late and you need to get your rest for the night. Settle down and get to sleep. You too Caladur. You can take the floor over here tonight." She indicated a mostly dry corner.

"Thank you ma'am. For everything."

-10-

That night was miserable for Caladur. He quickly came to realize why everyone all but sprinted back to their homes in the slums when the rain came. No one had a way to get dry after the rain soaked deep into their clothes. The sun was gone and nothing kept the wet elf warm. He sat listening to the young children shiver inside the dark shack. At one point in the night, the girl crawled across the shack to snuggle up next to her mother, the young boy was quick to follow.

The thought of joining the small family's huddle crossed his mind, but he was already thankful enough that he had a place to stay out of the still down pouring rain. He didn't want to push his luck.

The night pressed on for long hours, not giving much rest to the young elf. After the rain stopped and the night chill persisted, the sun finally began to rise in the eastern sky. Caladur needed to get out of the shack and get moving, anything to get his blood flowing again. He also needed to find a place to dry his clothes. The elf thought that if he showed up to the tryouts in soaked clothing, he wouldn't have a chance of being picked for the position.

Caladur stood up in the quietest fashion he could. The thought of thanking Estine for helping him crossed his mind, but he didn't want to wake anyone up. They were sleeping like a family of cats, huddled closely together. The elf stalked his way out of the shack and back into the dim streets of Fatiil. Not many people were outside. It always seemed that the entire city became sluggish after a rain storm like the one they experienced the previous night. No one wanted to be outside in the muggy weather. Those who had the means to stay inside a temperate and dry home would. If Caladur had any choice to be held up inside a well-built home at the moment, he would take it, and no one would blame him.

To warm himself, he began jogging through the streets with no destination in mind. It was still early morning and he didn't need to be to the arena district until mid-morning at the earliest. He thought it would be most prudent to go through the market district in hopes that one poor shop keep would be setting up early and looking for some help.

He made his way to the city wall on the northeast corner of the city. He turned around and began strolling towards the arena district. The sun had risen and his clothes began drying. The process was slow, but at least it was occurring. Caladur continued walking towards the arena district until he came across an elderly half-elf setting up his shop and struggling with a large wooden crate filled with various trinkets to sell.

Caladur could tell a half blood from a mile away. Their ears came to a short, rounded point unlike any other race he had ever seen. Their hair was almost always dark brown, sometimes black, rarely blonde. This particular man had shaggy black hair that housed streaks of grey. The other identifying characteristic of a half elf was their physical silhouette. Their body would frequently be built like that of a human. Bulky and somewhat disheveled, when compared to the physical posture of an elf. The head of a half elf however frequently appeared similar to the head of a full blood elf. Soft features accented in a near perfect way by a fine bone structure.

Caladur did not let the opportunity pass and quickly moved towards the man to lend a hand. With the elf's help, the shop keep was able to lift the crate up to his cart where he could properly examine the contents.

"Thank you Mr.," the shop keep began.

"Vandel. Caladur Vandel." He held out his hand to shake that of the middle aged man's. When his hand made contact, he realized that he was making a habit out of shaking hands with non-elves. First Owsin, then this man. And they both felt just like any elf's hand. Sure the man's hand was rough and calloused from years of hard work to provide for his family, but it was just like any handshake he had experienced with the elves.

"Well thank you Caladur. It's a pleasure to make your acquaintance."

"Mine too."

Caladur began to continue his walk towards the arena district when the man spoke again. "Caladur. You seem like you could use a little help, and obviously I need some. How about we make an arrangement? You come over here every morning to help me set up my shop, and I'll toss a few coins your way." The man smiled. He was still able to set up the shop by himself, for at least a little while longer until his age took too much of a toll, but his heart went out to the helpful elf wearing drenched, dirty clothing.

"You've got yourself a deal. I'll be here around sunup tomorrow. Ready to help. Is there anything else you need right now?" Caladur offered selflessly.

"I'll be fine today. But come ready to work for a couple hours tomorrow. I'll have some things for you to work on."

The men shared in another handshake before Caladur continued on his way to the arena district which, to his surprise, was packed full of people already. As he pushed through the crowds, he came to realize that well over one thousand people had come out to the arena to compete for the position of Rundor's apprentice. He began sizing himself up against the different people he saw waiting anxiously for the competition to begin. Most he felt comfortable besting in any of the three competitions he expected to participate in. Based on the bard, he was prepared to show off his agility, his strength, and his endurance. He had felt fairly comfortable in succeeding in each task, but he did not feel as though he would be able to best everyone outside of the arena. Most of those gathered appeared to be homeless, poor, or on their last leg. Many appeared to be malnourished, and although Caladur was headed there, he was still better off than most of those gathered. Then, there was a group of people dressed in fine clothes. They were well fed, well equipped, and ready to secure their position. Caladur knew that those people would be his biggest competition. They appeared to know what they were doing, the others seemed to be mostly clueless.

The hours crawled by as the crowed grew like a man's addiction to Ithexar. Now, at midday, there were approximately two thousand hopefuls awaiting their chance to prove that they were the best qualified to train under Rundor and compete in the arena. At last, just after the sun passed by the middle of the sky, the massive crowd began to quiet as loud trumpets announced the entrance of the arena's long standing favorite, Rundor.

Caladur struggled to make his way through the mass of people but was met with block after block of bodies also trying to squeeze through in order to get a glimpse of the famous warrior. After a few minutes of being pushed forwards and backwards through the crowd, he gave up and just stood in the crowed, realizing that soon enough he would be able to see the man he was competing for.

The trumpets blew again, all commotion ceased. The silence was almost eerie. He had never heard such a commotion die out with such speed. Then, over the crowd, an impossibly loud voice shouted. "You have all gathered here because you each feel you have something special to offer. Yet only one will be chosen. Over the course of these tryouts, all but one of you will fall. Many of you will face fear and injury head on. Some of you who prove yourself worthy enough to make it towards the end of the competition may even face death as you risk your life in battle. I strongly urge anyone who is not willing to put their personal health on the table for a chance to be my apprentice to quit now. If you do, hold your heads high, there is no dishonor in preserving your safety."

A few people here and there left the crowd but the mass stood firm, awaiting their first task.

"Those of you wise, or foolish, enough to stay will begin your tryouts immediately. The first test will be one of endurance. It is quite simple. Proceed to the western gate of the city. From there you will begin your run to the north, around the city wall. Continue your journey until you make it successfully back to the western gate. Along your way, there will be other members from the arena handing you a necklace and giving you a piece of advice which I would highly recommend considering. The first one hundred people to make it around the city and turn in their necklaces will be admitted to the next round. I will meet with those fortunate contenders here tomorrow at the same time. Best of luck to you all in your endeavor. The tryouts begin now!"

With another blow of the trumpets, chaos broke loose in the streets of the city as the hopeful apprentices made a mad dash towards the western gate. The city guard had the streets cleared between the arena and the gate so that no un-expecting citizen was stampeded by the mass.

Caladur began to make his way towards the gate but was unable to move very well. He was still in the midst of a crowd with very little room within which to maneuver. People were falling to the ground and begin trampled as the uncaring mass continued pressing relentlessly towards the gates.

Fifteen minutes later, Caladur got a breath of fresh air as the mass thinned and spread out in the open fields outside the city's wall. The elf made his way to the outside of the pack and began running at a good pace. He could clearly see that he was not the fastest, but it appeared to him that most of the people passing him were not running at a rate they could sustain over the entirety of the race. He continued clipping along in the countryside of Rostanlow.

Fatiil was situated within a large plain of the country. Sparse forests surround the city in almost every direction. Tall mountains were far to the west and could be seen only on exquisitely clear days. The air had warmed up and as Caladur's clothes dried on the outside, his sweat began to moisten the inside. He wondered if he would ever have on a clean, dry suit of clothes again.

After almost an hour of running, he came across an ornate shrine and decided that it must be the first stop for the race. The number of runners had declined by a significant amount in the past fifteen minutes. Many of those at the tryouts were unable to run for more than thirty minutes, let alone an entire afternoon. The city was large and would take even the fastest runners three hours to encircle. Caladur was happy with his pace and stopped only to visit the warrior at the first shrine. The shrine was decorated almost exclusively with deep blues. Even the champion was wearing dark blue clothes with lighter blue accents. Underneath the clothing, the champion was short, lean, and visibly quick. Although he stood motionless as the runners approached, Caladur had no doubt that he could move with the speed of lightning and the accuracy of a snake attacking its dinner. Caladur approached the champion with seven other runners who were keeping pace with him.

"Hello contestants. This is the shine of dexterity. In order to be the next apprentice, you must be as fluid as the air and as fierce as rolling water. You will soon need to overcome a task that displays your nimbleness and speed. Unless you want to be removed from the competition, you must complete the task with poise. Here is your prize for completing this leg, take it now and continue. The other shrines await your visit."

The champion handed each of the seven men a string necklace with a blue stone attached. Each runner put on the necklace and quickly resumed their run around the city of Fatiil. Along the way, two of the seven runners with Caladur fell behind. Only six remained as they rounded clockwise around the large city. The six runners did not share a word with one another as they continued their race. After another hour of running, another shrine appeared. This one was red.

Caladur picked up his pace to ensure that he was leading the group to the red shrine.

"This is the second stop," the brute-like human stated plainly. His red garb enhanced the muscles and tone of his chiseled body. "Here's your necklace. Red symbolizes the strength of fire. Keep it up and finish the race."

Caladur put on his necklace and didn't waste another moment at the shrine. He found the difference between the first and second shines almost laughable. Both men were champions in the arena but couldn't have been more different. With two necklaces secured around his neck, he was sure that he would be able to finish the second half of the race. He picked up his pace slightly and left another two of the contestants behind him as he continued running through the countryside of Fatiil. The day's temperature had risen significantly forcing Caladur to remove his shirt which he tied around his waist without stopping to think about it.

Caladur and three other runners came upon the third shine at the same moment. This shrine was green. The champion awaiting their presence was tall and muscular, but not like the champion at the red shine whose muscles were bulging underneath his clothes. The green champion's muscles were lean and toned. They appeared to be prepared for extended periods of exertion, not fast, explosive instances. The green shine also housed ten chairs which the champion invited the runners to sit in. One member from Caladur's group took the offer while the other three refused, making the one feel uncomfortable.

"Welcome racers, you are almost done. Take a moment to catch your breath before you continue your journey towards becoming the next apprentice. I can't tell you your exact place, but I can assure you that if you complete the race at this pace, you will be one of the top one hundred. Now take the green necklace of endurance. The green signifies the rich and lasting beauty of the earth. Take a moment to look upon nature before you endure the remainder of the race."

Caladur turned to look towards where the champion was motioning as he put on his third necklace. He hadn't realized the beauty that surrounded Fatiil. The shine was situated on the top of a small cliff face that overlooked the top of an endless expanse of green. The grass and the trees that composed the forests and plains below were breathtaking to him. A moment later, after catching his breath, he turned back to continue on his way to the finish line. He came to realize the other three runners who were with him were already a good way on with the race and hadn't taken the time to consider nature as the champion suggested.

"Keep it up," the green champion urged, "You're almost done."

Caladur took the encouragement and began running at his steady pace once more. He focused on the beauty of the world as he continued running towards his goal. On his way to the final checkpoint he passed two of the runners he had been with. One was walking and the other was jogging at such a slow pace, it may have been better for him to simply walk. It had been ten minutes since he saw anyone else when he spotted a purple shine in the distance. He drew near realizing it was not the end, but simply another checkpoint. He did not grow downhearted but continued to smile as he came to the shrine.

Within the purple tent sat an elderly woman. She looked towards the single runner and uttered one word. "Forty-two."

Caladur stood speechless unsure of the meaning. The woman appeared to be frail underneath her royal purple dress, yet her face seemed to be lively.

"You are the forty-second racer to pass by my way today. Take this purple necklace and remember that wisdom and clarity are the most important attributes of a champion. In order to succeed in this task, you must keep your wits. The purple represents the union of heat and coolness to combine a perfect union of the two. Wear this pendant with pride and you will surely become Rundor's apprentice. Now you've but one short leg of the race to complete, I know that you will be able to finish as long as you keep your head on straight and keep your mind set on the prize. Best of luck to you."

Caladur accepted the fourth and final necklace before resuming his run towards the finish line, the western gate of Fatiil. He was tired. He had been running for nearly four hours straight. The sun's heat began to cool as the sun made its way ever so slowly towards the western horizon. Caladur pondered the various types of challenges that laid before him as he continued on his way.

Then, faster than his life had turned upside down in the past week, his world flipped and he found himself on the ground with a man on top of him. The man had scraggly blonde hair, jumbled teeth, and horrible breath. A fist came across Caladur's face. Then another.

-11-

Caladur woke up on the outside of Fatiil. He had no idea how long he had been out. It couldn't have been too long, but the man with jumbled teeth was gone. The elf stood back up, regained his bearings and continued to run towards the gate of the city. With every step he took, his head pounded with pain. The man who tackled him was sure able to punch with solid force. The elf did his best to push the pain out of his mind while he took in the view and the fresh air as he trotted towards his goal.

Moments later, he found himself gazing upon the gate of the city. A few people were gathered, but there was no shrine as Caladur expected to find. He hustled towards the gate to find another champion from the arena waiting. This champion was dressed in his armor, as if he was prepared to enter the arena to fight.

"Hello," Caladur said as he approached the champion.

"May I help you sir?" The champion asked, somewhat confused.

"Am I in the top one hundred?" He was hopeful.

The champion looked Caladur up and down. "You would be number 85, but since you do not possess the four necklaces, I am afraid I cannot count you as a finisher."

Caladur grabbed frantically around his neck for the four necklaces he had been awarded. They were gone. "But someone stole them. He attacked me and took the necklaces."

"Look, I don't have the time or patience for cheaters. Now I'm sorry but without the necklaces, I cannot permit you to continue competing in this competition."

Without thinking twice, Caladur turned his back on the champion and began a sprint towards the purple shine. He thought to himself that she would remember him and that she could vouch for his completion of the race. On his way to the woman, he passed fourteen runners headed towards the finish line with all four necklaces. He made his way to the shrine just as another runner was spotted in the distance, approaching the final shrine. The runner would be the one-hundredth runners to cross the finish line if Caladur did not straighten things up and get to the finish.

"What happened to you?" The woman dressed in purple expressed her concern while Caladur was still approaching from a distance.

"Someone jumped me, knocked me out, and stole my necklaces. The champion at the finish said that I cannot pass on without all four necklaces. Is there anything you can do?" He was out of breath.

The older woman brought her hand to her chin to

think for a moment. "I believe that if you take my necklace to the champion, he will allow you to stay in the competition." She began unclasping a large, elegant necklace filled with stones of the four colors, blue, red, green, and purple. The center stone was purple. It was large and gave a sparkle that matched that of the brightest stars in the night sky when held just right in the late day's sun. On either side of the stone were smaller, but still large, stones. One was red, the other was blue. Encircling the three stones were small green jewels that glittered as the sunlight bounced through the precious stones. "Be sure that I get this back at the end of the day. I'll come looking for you in the arena district, where the race began. Can you manage that?"

"Yes ma'am. Thank you." Caladur was ecstatic. He didn't believe that he would be given another chance. He expected his journey to be done when he realized the necklaces had been stolen. He said, "Thank you," one last time before he once again resumed his run towards the western gate of Fatiil.

"Hurry up, this man here is number one hundred. If he beats you, there will be little I can do." She called after him.

Caladur picked up his pace. He knew exactly how far the finish was and exactly how little energy he had left. He paced himself and ran. With every step he found himself closer to his goal. He could see the city gate and the champion awaiting the final contestant to make the cut. His competitive nature forced his head to look backwards. He saw a man, a human, chasing after him. He had four necklaces bouncing up and down around his neck with each step he took. The gap between the two was closing as they both neared the finish.

Caladur began sprinting, giving the race everything he had. The other racer was still gaining. The champion stood up at attention as the two men were sprinting towards him. The gap steadily closed. Caladur pressed on harder and faster until he passed the champion. A split second later, the other man passed.

The elf fell to the ground gasping for air. The race had been completed. He just had to hope that the champion accepted the purple woman's necklace as a proper token of completing the race.

"You again?" the champion sneered. "I told you that you were not to come around again."

"I know." Caladur gasped for more air. "The purple champion," deep breath, "gave me this. Said it would count." Another gasp. "If you doubt me, ask her yourself." He resumed his panting, hoping with all of his pounding heart that the guard would accept the ornate necklace.

The champion looked Caladur up and down. He noted the necklace and the bruised face. "Alright. You're in. Congratulations. You are the final participant in this audition." The armored champion handed Caladur a thin slab of stone about as big as his hand. A picture of an arm, complete with bulging bicep, holding onto a snake could be seen. "Don't lose the stone. You won't be this lucky again." He turned towards the human who was also lying on the ground gasping for air. "I'm sorry sir. But you just missed the cut off. Feel free to register as a single fighter with the arena if you wish to fight. You look like you might fare well."

The man sighed and closed his eyes in utter disappointment. He lost out on his dream by less than a foot. And there was nothing he could do to change that. The man stayed outside of Fatiil dwelling on his defeat until after the sun set. He then made his way back to his home where he was welcomed by his wife and three children.

Caladur thanked the guard for accepting his story after taking a sufficient amount of time to catch up on his breathing. He then made his way back to the arena district where he waited for the purple champion to return. People moved every which way around him working on their daily business taking no notice of Caladur, the elf who was no longer an elf. Then, he spotted Oranton and Aervaiel in the distance coming his way. The two were holding one another's hand as they walked. Their graceful gait through the crowds made it appear as if they weighed nothing.

Caladur turned his back to the pair, ashamed to be in such a place, associating with this type of people. To his delight, the couple did not take notice of him and continued on their way through the slums to their homes.

"There you are."

The young elf almost jumped when a hand appeared on his shoulder. He quickly calmed when he realized the hand belonged to the purple champion.

"Congratulations. I spoke to the gatekeeper, he said he permitted you to continue in the competition. Good for you."

"Thank you," he replied as he removed the necklace from his neck. "Here you go, I really appreciate what you did for me."

"It was nothing. You deserved to finish the event. Now just keep up the dedication and you just might become the next champion of the Fatiilian arena."

As quickly as the purple champion appeared, she disappeared. She blended back into the crowd of people entering and exiting the arena, taking part in the day's activities.

With a great bit of relief, Caladur sighed to himself. One day of competition was complete. He had until midday tomorrow to return to the arena district. The young elf made his way back to the slums for the night, hoping that Estine would allow him to stay in their shack again. He didn't want to make a habit out of it, but for now, he had nowhere else to go.

The elf knocked on the door to the shack and waited with the patience of a child before he knocked again a few seconds later. He paused and heard a bit of scuffling on the wooden floor of the shack, but no one came to the door. "Estine?"

Silence from the shack for another moment before a voice resounded. "Caladur? Is that you out there?"

"Yes. Estine? May I come in?"

A moment later, Estine opened the door to grant Caladur admittance. "I thought it was only for one night," she stated in a clear, concise sentence.

"I had hoped it would be only one, but the arena isn't providing any,"

"Arena?" Estine exclaimed. "Did you run the race today?"

"Yeah. I finished in the top one hundred. I would have finished earlier, but some guy knocked me out and took the tokens I needed to complete the race. That's what this is from," Caladur pointed towards the bruise that was now a deep purple on his jaw. "But I finished. They mentioned providing a place to stay throughout the tryouts, but I guess I'll need to pass the next trial before I'm eligible for the housing. Just one more night would be greatly appreciated."

Estine looked the elf over. "Congratulations on making it through the first round. I've never known someone who has passed the first test. I'd be honored if you stayed here for the night. However, if you sleep here tonight, I require two things in return. The first is that you continue staying here through at least the end of the tryouts. I know Lucas will thoroughly enjoy hearing stories of the tryouts. He's dreamt of becoming a champion ever since he could talk. I also would ask that if you do become Rundor's apprentice, you grant my family admission to the arena whenever you are fighting so we can watch. Can you manage that?"

Caladur almost said no. He didn't want the slums to become his permanent home. The leaky roof, the uncomfortable floor, the close quarters. None of these aspects of the slums appealed to him. But there was one thing that outshone the negatives. The chance to be part of a family, even if he was just the random elf the family who had nothing took in, he would again be part of a community. "Yes. I'll stay here with you."

-12-

The night in the slums was actually enjoyable. His clothes were dry, it was not chilly, and the draft that went through the shack, in fact, helped sooth his burnt skin. It wasn't until late that night that he realized his entire back and chest were sore to the touch. Running the race without a shirt on took its toll on his now red torso.

The morning arrived and Caladur began making his way across the city towards the small shop he agreed to help set up. The middle aged man was waiting for Caladur to arrive. "Good morning to you Mr. Caladur. I trust yesterday treated you well."

"It did. I'm competing for Rundor's apprenticeship."

"So you ran the race?" Everyone in the city had heard about the race. With all of the commotion the previous day it was all but impossible to live in the city and be oblivious to the fact that the apprenticeship trials were taking place.

"Yes sir. I finished and am moving onto the next round. I don't know what I'm getting myself into. I think it'll only get more difficult."

"That'd be a safe bet," the man laughed

"So what do you need me to do today?"

"A little bit of this, some of that, and a whole slew of stuff in between." The man led Caladur into his shop.

The shop was called *Sutur's This's and That's*. Unlike most shops in Fatiil, the man's shop had a large window in the front displaying shelves full of merchandise. The shop's name's ambiguity was perfect for the mishmash of items populating the cluttered shop. In addition to the shelf in the front of the store, the walls were full of shelves supporting the weight of every item for sale.

"What is it that you specialize in, Mr. Sutur?" Caladur guessed at the man's name based on the shop's sign.

"Anything and everything. The people who come to shop here aren't looking for anything in particular. Many will come through every now and then simply for the experience of seeing the items I've managed to get into my inventory. For most people, it's the novelty of coming into a store like this. However, if people come in, they usually leave with something new, and a few less coins." While he explained, he walked Caladur around the store highlighting various objects of interest. Everything from storage barrels and chests in all sizes to ornate jars he claimed were fashioned in other lands, far from Rostanlow. Caladur had his doubts but didn't raise his concerns. "What I need from you first is just to straighten the place up. With so many people in and out, everyone touching something, or everything, the shop gets cluttered quickly. If you wouldn't mind straightening the items on the shelves, I would be appreciative. There's no particular order, just make it look neat. Can you manage that?"

Caladur nodded.

"Splendid. I'll be in the back, come get me if a customer arrives. It's rare for anyone to come this early, but business is business no matter the time." Mr. Sutur left Caladur alone in the front room as he began rearranging the clutter.

Caladur started his work with the front display case. The most unique items in the shop were crowded inside the display case in hopes to draw the attention of possible buyers. Uniquely shaped pieces of pottery that were brightly colored sat on the bottommost shelf required little attention. The next shelf was full of stones and fossils. Nothing too awe inspiring. The fossils were of plants or small animals, and the stones were not of any true value, they were however cut uniquely into various basic shapes and smoothed. Further towards the top of the shelves were assorted miniature statues and models. Most were made out of a type of metal, some were wooden, and others were carefully crafted out of obscure materials. The models were of everything. One was of the Fatiilian bastion, another of the arena, both were remarkably accurate. Most were of unnamed people. Mostly human, but a few elves and gnomes were scattered throughout the collection.

He spent about an hour on the front shelf alone. Arranging and rearranging the merchandise. The rest of the store took another hour. By the time he was done, it was getting to be about time to walk towards the arena district for the next day of tryouts. "Mr. Sutur?" He called towards the back.

A scuffling of feet sounded for a moment before the man appeared with a bright smile on his face. The dazzling appearance dissipated into a more natural expression when he realized there was not a customer in the store. He took a look around the place and clapped his hands together a few times. "Good job Caladur. The shop hasn't looked this great in quite a while. I'm sure it'll bring a few more people into the store. Good job indeed."

"Thank you sir." Caladur was awed by his own words. He never thought it would be so easy to associate with non-elves. Yet he had been succeeding splendidly ever since he was let out of jail. His thoughts ran rampant as he pondered what life would have been like if he didn't have the week in prison to process the struggles he was going through, if he had never met Owsin. He needed the time to stomach the idea of working with humans and beggars. Now, it seemed perfectly normal, as if he had never known life within the Order. Reality snapped back. "I do think I must be going, so I'm not late to the tryouts."

"Alright. Great job. I truly mean it. I'll see you here again tomorrow."

"Yes Mr. Sutur. I'll be here."

"I look forward to it. Now off with you, don't be late."

With one last goodbye, the young elf was back in the streets of Fatiil on his way to his second day of tryouts.

-13-

Caladur stood within the crowds outside of the arena for just under an hour while ensuring that he held the stone he was awarded yesterday in his fist. At last, the trumpets sounded again, in the same fashion they did the previous day. Many of the people in the streets quieted as the gnome bard began speaking in a tone loud enough for Caladur to make out the words.

"The race you've already won
But your tryouts have just begun
Four more trials await
Til the winner knows his fate
Purple, green, red, and blue
Are the colors you must each pursue
The tryouts will continue inside
Please only come with all your pride

Hand your stone to the ticket taker
Only come if you're not a faker
For if you try but have no stone
You'll be sentenced to a cell alone
So let the tryouts now resume
It's already getting close to noon."

The announcement ended. Caladur immediately began making his way towards the ticket taker of the arena he had never been to. Now that the stone was public knowledge, he knew he needed to protect it more than ever. A mass of people began making their way directly to the entrance, many more than the one hundred that had been permitted to continue competing in the tryouts. His grasp on the stone was so tight that he almost cut his hand while he squeezed. Then, after a good deal of pushing, shoving, and screaming, he arrived at the ticket taker.

"Spectator or participant?" The young man yelled over the roar of the mass.

Caladur held up the stone in his vice gripped hand.

"Participant. You're going that way." The man indicated to his right. Caladur fought to get to a small door beside the large entryway to the arena proper. As he passed through the door he felt like he was being taken to his jail cell again. A stone corridor of steps leading downwards guided Caladur towards a room that smelled of death. He restrained himself from pinching his nose in fear that a champion would see him and make an example of the elf.

The memories of looking at the arena champions as thoughtless brutes flashed back into his head. He didn't belong in the arena. His place was at the True Elf Rings with the other members of the Royal Order of True Elves, not competing for a position in this savage sport. He almost turned around to make his way out when he heard a voice.

"Do you know where the participants are supposed to go?"

Caladur looked around to see who was speaking before he laid eyes upon a man. The man had long, blonde hair. As he began to speak again, Caladur noticed that his teeth were jumbled around unlike any mouth he had ever seen. Then it hit him. It was the man that attacked him, knocked him out, and stole the necklaces. Based on the man's expression, he also recognized Caladur.

The thoughts of being too good for the arena abandoned him as he resolved to himself that he would do everything in his power to prevent the man who cheated and stole in order to make it this far from becoming Rundor's next apprentice.

The two men continued wandering the bowels of the arena without a word until they came across a large room filled with seventy or so other men. An older human boy, about seventeen years old asked both men to show their entrance stones. Both complied. They were then directed to take seats within the room as they waited for the rest of the participants to arrive.

Caladur took a seat near the front with an open seat on either side. He wasn't in the tryouts to make friends. He only needed two things. A steady income, and for the man with the messed up teeth to be knocked out of the competition.

After about thirty minutes of waiting, all one hundred contestants had taken their place within the room. Then, a man entered. He was tall, muscular, and had scars all over his face and exposed chest. He wore rugged looking pants that stopped just before his perfect, chiseled six-pack. His head was hairless and eyes seemed to survey the one hundred men awaiting their next challenge with a fierce interest. "Welcome back," he began. The voice was the same as the voice Caladur had heard yesterday before the race. "Congratulations on successfully completing the race. I have a few words for you all before I explain the next event in your training.

"It has been brought to my attention that at least one of you within the room has taken it upon themselves to cheat in the race yesterday. From what I understand, one of you only ran a very short part of the race and only had possession of the necklaces because you stole them from another contestant who gave their very best to rightfully complete the task. That said, if I see anyone, whether it is intentional or not, cheat at any point in these tryouts, I'll personally see to it that you never have another chance to cheat again.

"Now, with that bit of business out of the way, onto the next challenge. As you must have come to realize by now, there will be four areas that you will be tested in. They include strength, dexterity, endurance, and wisdom. As the days go by, the tests will become more difficult and dangerous. You each have the ability to bow out whenever you want. I understand. I would not be here today if I accepted every single challenge ever presented to me. Now. The challenge you will each face today will be a challenge of dexterity. This event will test both your aim and reflexes in one of the most basic ways.

"Go ahead and prepare yourself for the upcoming test. We'll be meeting in the Fatiilian Rings in a couple of hours. Please prepare yourselves for the test. I'll see you soon." Rundor took his exit from the room leaving the participants silent in his wake.

After a moment, the bustle began. Men turned towards one another to introduce themselves and share their theories about the specifics of the test. Caladur avoided conversing with the men and made his way out of the arena's dungeon.

Just over an hour later, Caladur found himself standing outside of the Fatiilian Rings. He recognized a few of the men entering the complex from the arena. Caladur made his way into the rustic looking building to join the other participants. He expected the inside to look similar to the True Elf Rings, however, the Fatiilian Rings was much larger. Caladur found Rundor and a large group of men within a roped off section of rings.

"After this challenge, only fifty of you will be left in the competition. Again, like the race, you will directly compete against one another. Please come up to find your name on this list and figure out which group you will be placed into. But before you do that, allow me to explain the rules. Your group will consist of five men. One at a time, you will take your spot on top of the ring while the other four men surround you. While on the platform, your job is to dodge the balls being thrown at you. For every ball you dodge, you will receive two points. Those of you on the floor will have four of these balls to hit the target with. For each hit you land, you will receive one point. Overall, the top fifty scorers will remain in the competition."

Caladur found himself in the fourteenth group. He observed the other groups to pick up any tips he could. He came to realize that he would need to accumulate about twenty four points to guarantee his spot in the next round. After about an hour, his group was called forward. He was the last one of the group to be on the stand, which he was happy to find. He expected the other four men to possibly wear their arms out, at least slightly, by the last round. At least that is what he had observed in some of the previous groups.

His group was called. Caladur approached the ring he was being called to and grabbed his first four balls. Each ball weighed about one pound of solid metal and was no larger and a person's fist. If one of the balls made contact with someone's head, there would be a significant chance for serious injury. Up to this point, no one had been hit in the head with one of the balls. Caladur waited for two of the other men to throw first before he made his first shot. The target was off balance and unable to dodge. 1 point.

The competitor continued utilizing his strategy of waiting to throw his ball until the target was distracted by another and it proved to be quite effective. When it was his turn to stand on the platform he had already gained eleven points. Caladur knew he had a good shot of making it through to the next round if he was able to dodge seven of the sixteen balls. The elf took his spot on the podium having already noted the strategies of the other men in his mind and prepared his body to react fast and move even faster. The first ball was launched and dodged without a problem. The next came immediately after, just missing Caladur's head. The balls continued for a moment. Ten balls had been thrown, six still remained. He had already dodged seven balls putting his total points up to twenty five points. The next onslaught of metal balls began. He dodged the first by ducking just a bit. Twenty seven points. Then a ball struck Caladur in the back of his head. His vision became constricted and his reactions were hindered. He stumbled a bit. The throwers didn't miss out on the opportunity. Of the remaining four balls, three hit. The only reason the fourth ball missed was due to the fact that the thrower was unable to aim with any sort of accuracy. Caladur didn't keep track of everyone's score, but he was quite sure that the man with the horrible aim scored less than ten points throughout the entire trial.

The event was over. Caladur had received twenty nine points. He was positive that he had performed better than half of the men and was guaranteed a spot in the next round. The elf took a seat on the floor with the other observers and rested as he held his head which was flaring with dull pain. For a few moments darkness constricted his vision, but after a brief threat of unconsciousness, Caladur regained his full sight.

About an hour later, the competition had ceased and the points had been tallied. Many of the contestants who scored under ten points had already left the facility with their dreams shattered. A few delusional men who scored under fifteen stuck around hoping that Rundor would see the fire in their hearts and give them another chance. Based on what Caladur had seen, Rundor was not the type of man to give second chances. You perform well the first time or you don't perform at all. You had to. After all, in the arena you would often be fighting for your life. The risky profession didn't make sense to some, but within Fatiil, the champions held a position of honor within the city. Caladur was slowly beginning to learn this.

Rundor raised both of his muscular arms into the air silencing the men. "If you scored above twenty-four points you will be admitted to the arena tomorrow at midday. If you are unsure of your score, don't bother asking, or coming back. Those of you who succeeded in this task are welcome to go to the arena's barracks for a meal and some care, I'll see you tomorrow." The champion took his leave from the Fatiilian Rings and the men followed. Most were happy, others were down-heartened. Caladur was more than excited. He had passed the second round of cuts.

The elf made his way amongst a number of other participants who passed the test to the barracks of the arena. It was a place most people never get the chance to enter. While entering the barracks, a champion of the arena instructed the men that rooms had been prepared for each of them if they desired. The thought appealed to Caladur and he almost jumped at it before he recalled the promise he had made to Estine and her children. Although the room that was being offered was sure to be protected against the elements and most likely more comfortable than the shack in the slums, Caladur rejected the offer.

The small hall of the barracks housed large tables that were flooded with more than enough food and drink for the men who made their way to the next round. The walls were covered with various banners and flags representing the diverse champions who had found their untimely deaths while fighting in the Fatiilian arena. Besides the greeter, the hall seemed to be empty of champions. Caladur thought that they must have left the hall in order to avoid associating with the young hopefuls who would bombard them with worthless questions. Caladur didn't take time to eat a leisurely meal like some of the other men. Rather, he quickly ate some food by himself at the end of one of the tables. He could overhear the other men discussing what the next trial may be. The elf thought to himself, "what good will postulating on the next trial be when there was no way to be sure?" He laughed a bit to himself. After he finished his meal, he packed some food for Estine, Lucas and Celeste in a sack provided by the arena and made his way home. Back to the slums.

-14-

The night came and went. To Caladur's surprise, Estine and her children did not come into the shack at any point during the night. His heart filled with concern for the family of beggars he barely even knew. The family of humans had found a place within Caladur's heart even though they had shared less than a hundred words with one another. Morning came and Caladur left, attempting to convince himself that the family was safe and just happened to be caught up somewhere else. He was aware of the horrible things some people would do to the homeless of Fatiil. He did, after all, use to be one of the spineless jerks who tortured the less fortunate.

Just as the sun began to brighten up the morning sky, the young, beaten elf entered *Sutur's This's and That's*. He found Mr. Sutur sitting on a chair behind the counter sipping on a cup of steaming tea. "Good morning Caladur.

Can I get you a glass?" As Mr. Sutur approached the elf, he noticed the bruises on Caladur's exposed skin that had been accumulating over the past two days of tryouts. "You look like you could use one."

"Thank you sir. That sounds fantastic."

A moment later the hot tea warmed the clay cup which warmed Caladur's hands. He sighed and closed his eyes. It had been over ten days since he last enjoyed the feeling of a warm beverage surging down his mouth and into his stomach. The scent of the tea was glorious. A warm, sweet aroma filled his nostrils making him forget that he was at the shop to work, not to relax. One more sip from the tea. "What do you need from me today?"

"Tidy up the front room just like yesterday, it should go by much quicker with only one day's worth of passerbyers. When you're done, let me know and I'll show you the back room. Oh, and if a customer comes in, just give me a holler."

"Yes sir," the elf said as he set down his tea on the counter and began working.

The man was right. He wondered how long it had gone untouched before he came along to help. With only one day of traffic through the store, he was able to get everything together in less than an hour.

While he was putting the finishing touches on a shelf full of brightly colored rocks, a young human girl entered the shop. Caladur was sure he had seen her somewhere before but couldn't place her. Her long, dark hair was oddly attractive to the elf who had only ever been allowed to court those with perfectly blonde hair. The girl took no notice of the elf and began perusing the neatly organized merchandise.

Caladur watched her move gracefully through the shop out of the corner of his eye, trying to keep his interest in her unnoticed. To his knowledge, he succeeded. After a moment, he went into the back room to summon Mr. Sutur.

The girl spent about ten minutes in the shop before buying a few statues from the front display case. Caladur watched intently as Mr. Sutur helped the girl find everything she was looking for, bartered a proper price and completed the sale. Mr. Sutur wished the girl a good day and opened the door for the customer on her way out.

"Take good notes?" Mr. Sutur asked once she was away.

Caladur laughed silently to himself. "Mental notes."

"Good. One of these days, you might be making the sales. Now then, are you about done?"

"Yeah. I was just finishing when she came into the shop. What do you need me to do now?" He asked eagerly, ready to help his employer out.

"I've got some stuff in the back. Follow me."

The back storeroom was much larger than he expected to see. Piles upon piles of crates filled the room. Small aisles were all that separated one stack of crates from the next. It looked organized, but it would have been all but impossible to retrieve any specific crate without a great deal of work.

"Well, this is the rest of my inventory. It's all carefully organized and packed away until I need to put the items out front. As you can see, I went a little overboard about a year ago with my purchases. But it'll all sell, as soon as there is space for it in the front," the man gave a chuckle. "What I need is to get the crates into an order so that when it's time to put another crate out in the store, it'll be a crate with a different type of items. That way the shop won't be flooded with the same stuff and there is a variety of trinkets for the buyers to peruse. I've been making a list of the crates and how I want them ordered. As you've seen, it's difficult for me to move a single crate, let alone an entire storeroom full of them. I don't expect this to be done today, just get it done as quickly as possible. Sound good?"

"Yes sir," the enthusiasm that dripped off of his words was completely superficial. The task was daunting in the least. Even, impossible. But it's all that Caladur had to occupy his time with. The old man was nice enough too. He wasn't unbearable like he expected most humans to be. In fact, he hadn't really come across a single human that pushed his buttons in a way that was particularly unfavorable since his excommunication from the Royal Order of True Elves. Less the man that stole his necklaces in the race, of course, but just the one.

Caladur began working to the best of his ability, trying to follow the directions that were jotted down on the piece of parchment Mr. Sutur had given him. After a couple hours of rearranging the crates, his quitting time came. As he made his way out of the shop, Mr. Sutur stopped him and gave him two things. The first was a smile, full of thanks. The second was a pouch, full of pieces of copper and silver. After everything, Caladur had managed to make some money. "We'll see you tomorrow," he said as he exited *Sutur's This's and That's*. Caladur knew for certain what he was going to use the money for. But first, he had to return to the arena. With a new sense of happiness, he made his way to the arena, prepared to be torn apart in some new way. But all for a cause. This was all for a cause.

-15-

There were no more trumpets. Caladur simply made his way past the ticket taker and into the bowels of the arena, ready for the challenge of the day. The room he had been instructed to go to the day before was once again guarded by the human boy.

"Name please."

"Caladur Vandel," the elf responded.

"Your score?"

"Twenty-nine."

He checked a list, smiled, and said, "Head on in, please sit towards the front."

Only twelve other men were in the room. Over the next fifteen minutes, seven other men joined their ranks. Caladur began counting the men within the room. Then, his calculations were interrupted by a commotion at the door.

"What do you mean I'm not allowed in? I scored over a twenty-four." The door flew open and a middle aged man forced his way into the room with the boy following behind him.

"You didn't know your exact score. I'm under orders to only allow the participants whose name is on my list and know the number marked by their name. You said twenty-nine, but you had thirty points. Now I'm asking you one more time to leave." The human, despite his firm words, appeared to be in fear. The older man would have no trouble making quick work out of the boy.

The aggravated man took a seat on one of the benches in the auditorium as if nothing had happened. Everyone else stared at his face, which was flushed red with anger. After the boy took his post outside the door again, the man roared at the other participants, "What are you all gaping at?"

With that, everyone faced forward once more, ignoring the man.

A couple minutes later, another man was permitted entrance into the room. The blonde haired man with jumbled teeth entered, gave Caladur a sneer, and took a seat on a bench in the second row.

Rundor came into the auditorium through his entrance on the other side of the room. Forty-five participants awaited their instructions with eager anticipation.

"Congratulations to each of you. You've performed admirably over the past two days. But the fun's over. Today the stakes are going to be raised. You've been tested in your dexterity. Only strength, endurance, and wisdom remain. You must be proficient in each of these attributes in order to survive more than a day as a champion of the

Rundor's Apprentice

Fatiilian arena. In order to demonstrate how the stakes are being raised, I'll need one of you to help." Rundor paused for a moment as he perused the audience. "You sir, come on up here. What's your name again?"

"Wes."

"Good. Now Wes, what did you score in yesterday's event?"

"Thirty." He was confident. The boy had told him his actual number of points when he forced his way into the room defying the directions the arena's employee stated plainly to him.

"Splendid. Now, I would like you all to see exactly what I meant the other day. Wes, have a seat here please," he indicated a wooden chair. Wes sat. "I warned you all that any type of cheating or dishonorable activity would not go unpunished.

Wes lost his air of confidence, but kept his seat, in hopes that Rundor wasn't made aware of his actions. While he was seated, convincing himself that he was alright, Rundor's fist surged into his jaw. The punch was indescribable. It came with the force of a horse rearing back and coming down on a watermelon. Wes's jaw was dislocated, but he didn't have a chance to think about that before Rundor wrapped his arms in a hold around the injured man's neck, depriving his lungs of precious oxygen.

Once the man stopped struggling, Rundor released his grip. "No worries, he's alive and will be nursed to heath before being released. I hope you all take this lesson to heart. There will be no more dishonorable actions taken by any of you throughout the remainder of this competition. Did I make myself clear?"

The stunned men nodded, a few uttered a "yes," but most were speechless. Caladur looked towards the man who stole his necklaces. The elf watched as the jumbled toothed man gulped in discomfort. A dull pain was created in the pit of his stomach. In his mind, he replaced the beaten man with himself, unconscious in front of the other men. The page boy entered the room and dragged the unconscious body out, presumably towards the medical station, but the men couldn't be sure. Caladur never saw the man called Wes again.

"Today, well over the next couple days, we will be testing your endurance. As a champion, it is important to be able to keep in the fight for a long period of time. Battles I've been in have lasted anywhere between thirty seconds to just under an hour. We must be able to keep our strength up in order to win the fight. The test will take place at Lake Oznet, which is three day's travel away by foot. The training will begin in four days. Transportation will not be provided. You must each make your way to Lake Oznet. My page has a map for each of you and will give you each one on your way out." He surveyed the participants for a moment. "I'll see you all soon. Have a safe trip." Rundor left the room and began preparing for his own journey to Lake Oznet.

Caladur was in no hurry, but the other participants were. Most of the men rushed out of the room, eager to begin their journey to the large lake to the south of the city. Caladur had never been there, he really had never been far out of the city, but he was more than excited to have the opportunity to travel. He was the last to exit the room and collect his map from the young boy.

Back on the streets, Caladur knew he had business to take care of before embarking on his journey to the South. His first stop was Fatiil's bastion, a place he hadn't been to since he was discharged from the prison. Now, he felt like a completely different person.

"I've got bail money," Caladur told the guard manning the front desk in the large entrance hall.

"Right this way," the apathetic guard led Caladur down the familiar hallways to the pit that Caladur called his home for a week.

Caladur found himself being ushered down the hall off cells to the only cell inhabited by a prisoner. Behind the iron cage sat an old man with a grungy beard accented with clumps of dried dirt that dangled in the forest of his grey hairs.

"Where's Owsin?" Caladur asked the guard.

"Owsin? The guy who was here last week?"

Caladur nodded.

"I think his boy came by and bailed him out a couple days ago. I was off duty, but when I came in yesterday, he was finally gone. I don't think we've ever kept someone for so long for such a minor offense." The guard explained as he began ushering Caladur back towards the entrance of the bastion.

"Do you by chance know where he lives? I've got something for him."

"I certainly don't. You really think that I know the residence of every bit of riff raff that comes through here?"

Caladur realized that he was asking a lot of the guard. "I guess not."

The elf made his way back into the streets of Fatiil. He was disappointed that he was unable to help the man who helped him, but he was on a timeline, once he was a champion, he would have time to track Owsin down and pay him back for the gift. The gift an uneducated man gave the elf. Not the gift of freedom, but the gift of accepting people who weren't elves into his life.

The elf walked to *Sutur's This's and That's* in the pleasant summer sun. To his surprise, the shop was populated by a few people perusing the merchandise he took care to arrange earlier that morning. He hadn't experienced many people being in the shop with him, it felt almost out of place.

Mr. Sutur was happy to see his young employee enter the store and quickly made his way to the elf. "What brings you out here this afternoon?"

"I got some bad news. The tryouts are moving us down to Lake Oznet. I need to leave this afternoon and I won't be back for a week."

"That sounds great!" the older man was, without a doubt, excited to hear the news. He jumped a little and smiled broadly, reminding Caladur of Owsin. The few customers in the store took a step back, away from the store keep who was celebrating like a child who found a shiny gold piece on a street corner. "Why in the world could that be bad?"

"I'll be gone for a week. I won't be able to finish the storeroom."

"No worries. It'll be waiting for you when you get back. Good luck Caladur. You'll do fine."

"Thanks. But, while I'm here, there are a few things I'd like to purchase if you don't mind."

"Oh you don't need to," Mr. Sutur began.

"Yes I do."

Mr. Sutur stopped insisting, he could tell by the look on the elf's face that Caladur was going to pay for whatever he picked out, no matter what an old man said. "Fine," he conceded, "but I'm naming the price."

The elf nodded in agreement as he perused the shelves of merchandise he was wholly familiar with. It didn't take him long to select two perfect gifts. The first gift was a rag doll with yellow, string hair. A wide smile was stitched across the doll's face. The limp body had a blue dress with white polka-dots attached to the doll at the elbows and knees. Caladur then went to the glass display case where he had been putting a colorful top crafted out of iron. With the two toys in hand, he approached Mr. Sutur.

The shop keep looked over the merchandise and the two came to an agreement on the price. Once the transaction was settled, Mr. Sutur once again wished Caladur luck on his next trial and watched through the glass display window as the elf retreated to the slums of Fatiil.

Caladur was still concerned for the family he had stayed with for the past two nights. The elf remembered back to the last night when he stayed in the shack alone. The fear that Estine and the children would not be there grew within him with each step he took, but he pressed on. He walked through the slums, and to his delight, found himself watching Estine playing with her children outside of the shack. The relief hit him, releasing most of the tension his muscles held.

The young boy, Lucas, spotted Caladur first. He stopped playing with his mother and sister, and charged towards Caladur with a beaming smile. The boy jumped up into the air only to be caught by the elf who spun him around once before he set him back down. "We missed you."

"Where were you all?" He asked the young boy loud enough so his mother could hear.

"We stayed with my sister and her family for the night," Estine responded. "They enjoy our company from time to time, but don't have a large enough place for us stay permanently. Not that we would. This suits us just fine. What are you up to? We don't normally get to see you during the daytime."

"I'm still in the running for the apprentice. But we're heading south to Lake Oznet for the next test. I'll be gone for a week or so. I wanted to make sure you were alright. I missed you guys last night."

"Sorry about that. I almost came to tell you, but I didn't think you would really notice. I'll let you know next time. Have fun on your trip. And don't forget about us when you get back. We'll be right here." She laughed, "Lucas can't stop talking about you. He has to tell everyone we meet about your chance at becoming Rundor's apprentice." She smiled. "In fact, he wouldn't stop talking about you last night. My sister actually asked me to invite you over. Since you're leaving, I guess it'll have to wait until you get back. But when you do get home, they would be happy to meet you. Their daughter seemed interested in you too." The woman caught Caladur off guard when she winked.

"Sounds great. I'll let you know as soon as I'm back in the city. Hey," Caladur exclaimed as he remembered the toys he just purchased, "I got the kids something."

"You really didn't need to."

"I know. It's not much, but I thought they'd enjoy these." Caladur pulled the doll and the top out of his haversack. "Lucas! Celeste!"

The children ran over with beaming smiles. They both had already spotted the toys Caladur was trying to hide behind his back.

"Hey guys. I'm going away for a few days. But, before I go, I wanted to get you each a little something. Celeste, I got you this doll. I hope you like it."

The young girl grabbed the rag doll and began spinning around while holding the doll's hands. Her laugh was infectious and Caladur couldn't help but smile as the girl continued dancing and laughing with her new toy. He snapped out of it a moment later when he felt Lucas tugging on his shirt. "Don't worry buddy. I got you something too." Caladur took a knee on the gravel street, smoothed off of the surface so an area of firm sand sat uninterrupted. Not even by a pebble. He then spun the top with a flick of his wrist. The colors of the top began to blend together as it sped around in a small circle, leaving a shallow trail in the sand.

Once the top came to rest with its blue side upwards, Lucas picked up the toy and tried to spin it, but the top simply fell to the ground. The boy tried again, but the top fell again to its side. On his third attempt, the boy managed to make the top complete a full three hundred and sixty degree turn before it fell to the ground.

"Don't worry Lucas. You'll have it down to an art by the time I get back." Caladur stood up and roughed up the boys hair. "I guess I better get going." He looked towards Celeste once more to see her continually play with her doll.

As he was saying his goodbye to Estine, a rotten apple struck Caladur on the back of his head. He turned to survey where the piece of fruit came from, and found the source immediately. Oranton. His old best friend stood sneering.

"Enjoying the slums mixed blood?"

The voice, the tone, almost everything about it was familiar to Caladur. Before he had a chance to respond,

Lucas stood up tall and stared down Oranton. "You better take that back elf. Caladur's going to be a champion of the arena. He could turn you into a paste without even thinking about it."

Oranton began laughing.

Caladur's head dropped.

"You've resorted to the arena? Is that really all you could manage? I guess after all, you're blood doesn't qualify you for anything better. Living with slum scum and working in the arena. I can't believe I used to call you a friend." Oranton turned his back and continued walking through the slums until he felt an apple strike the back of his head. He turned and quickly ran towards Lucas with a monstrous ferocity. The elf towered over the young boy and grabbed him by the neck of his already tattered shirt. "You best watch yourself boy. Learn your terrible place in society and live with it. Next time I won't be so forgiving." As Oranton clenched his fist, the boy's shirt began to tear.

A moment later the neckband split and Lucas fell to the ground before he crawled away. Once a few feet separated the boy and the elf, Lucas ran to his mother with tears streaming down his face, terrified.

"I'm sorry," Caladur apologized, "That was my fault. He's a friend from the past. The distant past."

"No. Lucas needs to learn to control his temper. The elf was right. We are residents of the slums. My children need to learn how to behave in this level of society," she turned to Lucas and began scolding, "I don't want to ever see you do anything like that again. You're fortunate that the elf didn't hurt you. He could have done whatever he wanted to you and gotten off without any consequences." Her voice changed from scolding to caring. "I know it's hard. But this is our life right now. I'm doing everything I can to make all of our lives better."

The young boy nodded as tears continued flowing from his eyes.

After Lucas, Celeste, and Estine had all calmed down, Caladur said his goodbyes once more and made his way towards the southern gate of the city to begin his journey to Lake Oznet in order to continue his pursuit of Rundor's apprenticeship.

-16-

The journey to the lake was simple enough. A large trading road ran south and passed within a few miles of the lake. The map that was given to Caladur made the way clear. Take the trading route South for two and a half days, then, after passing through a small town called Ashwillow, take a turn onto a local path that led down into the valley where Lake Oznet sat.

His first night on the road was, to his surprise, somewhat pleasant. For the first time, he laid down beneath the stars and moon for a few hours while he meditated. The air was very cool and invigorating. It gave his body, which was healing bit by bit, relief from the hot summer sun. During his time of reflection, he focused on his experiences in the past two weeks. It seemed surreal. Not being a man released from prison and into the slums, but being a member of the Royal Order of True Elves. He thought for hours on how he could have wasted the first eighty years of his life on a group that would, with no second thought, turn its back on him. He laughed. Relief seeped through his pores as he came to find he was no longer held by the superficial codes of the Order.

It was on the morning of his second day of travel that he met up with another man he recognized. The man was easily the shortest man left in the running for Rundor's apprenticeship standing at a meek height of only five feet and some change.

"How's your travel going?" the man asked as he caught up to Caladur and made eye contact.

"Surprisingly well," Caladur replied. "It was a wonderful night last night and the morning seems to be shaping up well. How's your journey?"

"Fine. Just fine. Say, what's your name? I've not caught it yet."

"I'm Caladur," he offered his hand as the pair took part in an obligatory handshake. "And you?"

"Name's Tald. Nice to meet you Caladur."

The men shared an awkward silence as they continued walking southward. While Caladur took in the natural beauty he learned to value, it felt as though the other man was looking at him in a strange way.

"You're an elf." Tald finally blurted out almost five minutes later.

Caladur stopped walking, unsure how to respond.

"I mean, I'm surprised to see one of your kind taking part in this competition. Don't the elves disdain the arena?" He could tell by Caladur's response that he had hit a nerve deep within the elf. "I don't mean to pry," he reeled, "It was just something that came across my mind. Just something

I've always heard, you know, one of those stereotypes that get people into trouble. I didn't mean to," the man would have continued rambling for a while longer had Caladur not interrupted him.

"I'm not an elf." His voice was even. No emotion came with the words.

The single statement of fact shut the man up.

Caladur and Tald continued their journey throughout the rest of the day. They shared a few words with each other but spent much of the time silent. Tald realized he had hit a significant sore spot with the young "elf" and didn't want to cause any bad blood between himself and another competitor for the position. Caladur was happy to continue in silence.

The pair continued on their way towards Ashwillow. By midday, when the pair looked behind them they had lost sight of the city of Fatiil. Even, the unbelievably tall bastion had been devoured by the horizon. The loose pavement of the road wound southward over the plains of Rostanlow. A few hills rolled across the flat land, but they were distancing themselves from the mountains and descending bit by bit to the heart of the country.

The sun went down and Tald decided that it was time to rest for the night. The two men shared a brief goodbye as Caladur continued his journey towards the lake. He realized that as an elf, he had an edge on the other men. He was able to travel longer each day and make his way to Lake Oznet faster than anyone else.

Through the night, he passed by a number of camps. Some were comprised of families, others of a small number of the remaining participants pursuing apprenticeship. The night continued as did Caladur. In time, after midnight had come and passed, Caladur found a fallen tree and sat upon the trunk where he began his meditation for the night.

Morning came and he began his travel once more. The flat plains began to become populated by more hills as he approached the lake. Late in the morning, he spotted a small town in the distance. He surveyed the map and calculated the time traveled in his head before he came to the confident idea that it must be the town of Ashwillow.

He arrived in the town just before midday came about and was received with open arms. The small streets, which paled in comparison to those of Fatiil, were populated with a sparse number of the citizens of Ashwillow who came to welcome the visitors to the town. It was apparent that they were expecting the parade of hopeful champions to pass through their town. Young children fenced with sticks they pretended were swords as they imagined they were fighting in the fabled Fatiilian Arena, a place most of them had never had the luxury of seeing first hand. The married women watched over their children while their husbands were away, hard at work. Those women of Ashwillow who happened to be yet single gave Caladur becoming looks, a few of which made him blush. However, despite their advances, he passed each one as he continued through the town. The attention from the women jogged his mind back to the day he was being escorted to prison and he spotted an attractive human girl. Her picture filled his mind which rapidly created blissful thoughts of the human.

"Welcome to Ashwillow." His private moment was shattered. "You're the second to come by. How was your journey?" A nice looking man in his middle forties welcomed him in an energetic manner. After Caladur told a brief recap of his eventless journey, he was ushered further by the man. "The first contestant came through just a couple hours ago. I was surprised to see him ride in on a finely groomed horse. I was informed by Rundor that most of the remaining men came from little or no money. Either way, welcome. If you'll follow me, we've managed to secure a roof for your head tonight. It looks like a storm may be coming in. But then again, you can never be sure about the weather. Either way, you'll be in the courthouse with the other contestant, Yost was his name." He stopped outside of the largest building in the town. "He's inside waiting for company. If you need anything, please come find me. Best of luck to you, Caladur. You're expected at the lake tomorrow by midday. You'll have plenty of time if you leave in the midmorning tomorrow. Enjoy your stay in Ashwillow."

The man left Caladur to enter the courthouse alone.

The entrance room was large compared to the rest of the courthouse. A large desk sat in the center of the room about thirty feet away from the main entrance. Doors flanked either side of the desk secluding the offices of the officials of the town behind them. On the right side of the room sat a staircase that attempted to be elegant which led to a walkway above. The second floor of the town hall was populated by several doors. Behind these doors were small rooms furnished with uncomfortable beds and a small table with a cupboard beneath for the inhabitant's belongings.

While Caladur surveyed the room, his eyes fell upon Yost, the other hopeful apprentice who arrived in Ashwillow before him. He was accompanied by two of the women who welcomed him to the town. The elf recognized Yost right away as the human with the messed up teeth who stole his necklaces in the race.

Yost gave the women a flick of his hand dismissing them from the courthouse with a promise that he would find them later. Once the women were gone, he approached Caladur. "So you're the second to make it I assume."

"You made it first. How'd you manage to cheat this time?" Caladur's rage began to fill his body.

The man clicked his tongue against the roof of his mouth. "We mustn't tell our secrets elf. I've got mine, I'm sure you've got yours. Everyone who makes it this far has done something they're not too proud of. You and I alike. I'm sure." His words seemed to seep out from behind his teeth.

Caladur made no attempt to respond.

"Oh. Now don't go silent on me elf. You can't make me believe that you've been honest up to this point." He tried to place a hand on Caladur's shoulder.

The elf backed away.

"Aww. C'mon. You must have done something in order to finish the race. With me knocking you out and all, you must have pulled a few strings with your elven brothers. There's no other way for you to have finished. You're not that fast." A sigh. "But now that you've got me talking, I can't hold it in. On my first day of travel, I came across a man riding towards Fatiil on a fine looking horse. He didn't take the blade too well, but in the end, I won the horse and galloped my way here in a timely manner."

"You killed a man for his horse?" Caladur couldn't believe it. Beating a man up and stealing the necklaces was one thing, but killing? That was on an entirely different level. At least to Caladur it was.

Yost did not show any emotion. "I couldn't have him going to the guard to report me. Rundor would have taken me out of the competition without a thought. I'm not letting this opportunity slip by.

"You'll be caught if you keep this up. Doesn't that concern you?"

"I've not been caught yet. And I don't plan on ever being caught. I keep my misdeeds hidden. I don't tell anyone. In fact, you're the only person who knows about either of my transgressions throughout this little tourney." The brightness from his eyes disappeared and was replaced by darkness. "We can't have that, now can we?"

A shiver of fear ran through Caladur as he prepared for the impending fight.

"Why so tense?" The brightness returned. "I can't do anything here. They know you and I are the only people present. I would be done for. Besides, no one would believe you, even if you came out and told them of my transgressions. Now, be a good elf and get unpacked up in your room. The second one should suit you well." Yost offered his hand alongside a snide grin which Caladur walked right by as he ascended the stairs to his room.

-17-

Twenty-nine more hopefuls had arrived later in the day, before the festivities began. About an hour before sundown, Tald made his way into the town. He was welcomed, just like Caladur. However, he wasn't given a room in the town hall. Only the first three competitors who arrived were given a room there. The rest were given a bed with one of the townspeople. It served as a perk for only the first three men. They wouldn't be bombarded by curious townsfolk awestruck by the soon to be royalty staying in their home.

The sun began setting behind the western horizon, but the party was just beginning. It became apparent to Caladur that having the hopeful champions stay in their town was a big deal. When the sun set, Ashwillow came to life. The men were back from working the fields surrounding the small hamlet. The children were fed and ready to have a fun evening catching lighting bugs with their friends, and, if they were lucky, they would meet the next champion of the Fatiilian arena.

When the last bit of light left the warm sky, the nighttime darkness was illuminated by bright white sparks emitted from fireworks. These brilliant sources of exploding light were a rarity in Rostanlow, reserved only for the most special occasions. Caladur, in his eighty plus years of life had never had the opportunity to observe the wonder. The ROTE had more than enough money to purchase these miraculous items, but the Royal Order would never support the dwarves with their money. The dwarves, after all, were the only other race of Rostanlow that managed to keep their blood pure from other races. One wouldn't hear the elves of Rostanlow even mutter this, but the dwarves managed quite well. They kept their kind secluded to their majestic halls beneath the mountains. The sight of a dwarf, much like the sight of dwarven fireworks, was certainly rare.

After the light show, music began. The instruments were out of balance. The horns were loud, and the stings were too quiet to hear. The drums kept the rhythm for the band whose talent was easily surpassed by the homeless troubadours from the streets of Fatiil. Although the music was subpar, the people danced in the large square of the village. Caladur sat by himself on the side of the square, taking in the scene. His curious mind forced his eyes to watch Yost dance and flirt with the two women he was courting in the town hall when Caladur first arrived. The dancers spun around the square and after a short while, Yost was lost within the crowd.

"When did you get in?" Tald asked the elf while taking a seat on the bench next to him.

"Just before midday. They put me up in a room in the town hall. Where're you staying?"

"In a home. No bed, but they had a blanket laid out for me. I guess it'll have to do."

The men watched the townspeople dance for a moment.

"Why aren't you dancing?"

"I don't think my wife would appreciate it too much." Tald laughed. "She's not really the jealous type, but better safe than sorry. Anyway, tomorrow is an endurance test, so I want to conserve my energy tonight. You know?"

"Yeah."

"Especially if I need to sleep on the floor of a strange home."

The music played on and on. After a short while, many of the townspeople took a seat on the benches surrounding the square. The children were ushered to their homes to get some rest. The champions who were able to remember that they had a big day coming up began making their way towards their assigned locations. A number of the younger townspeople continued dancing, a few of the women made passes at the champions who hadn't yet left the celebration.

Two girls, who appeared to be sisters playfully walked towards Caladur and Tald just before the two men stood up to part ways for the evening. "You both champions?" The older of the two sisters asked.

"Yeah," Tald responded with a polite tone, "But we're on our way to bed for the night. Big day tomorrow."

Caladur nodded in agreement.

The two girls laughed. "Big day? For a short guy like you everyday must seem big."

The height difference between Tald and the girls became apparent to Caladur. Although he was as tall as the two girls, Tald was about six inches shorter.

Tald looked down the short distance to his feet while the girls continued to give attention to Caladur. The younger sister wrapped her hands around the elf's left arm and squeezed. "Do you need to go to bed now?"

Caladur struggled to state the response he had trouble formulating. "Yes."

After a bit more refusal, the two sisters left Tald and Caladur alone in an attempt to find a couple of more willing competitors.

"I hate short jokes," Tald exclaimed after a moment of awkward silence. "Can't people see past the fact that I'm short? I mean, I've lived with these jokes about my height since I was a kid. After twenty-seven years of them, they really get to wear on you. You know? My wife is taller than me. My kids are almost taller than I am. I just thought that competing for this position would put an end to them, but even now they're still coming." Tald's rant ended.

Caladur didn't respond. He found the girl's joke somewhat funny. But he wouldn't let his new fiend know that. He could see that it hurt him. "Hey Tald," Caladur said with an upbeat inflection. "How about you take my room in the town hall tonight."

"What?"

"Stay in the town hall. You won't need to deal with the questions from the people you stay with. You'll have a comfortable bed. Well, *a* bed. You'll get a better night of sleep."

"What about you?"

"I'll be fine. I'm going to stay outside tonight. It's beautiful. Anyway, I don't need to sleep the whole night. I only need to trance for a while. A perk of being an elf."

Caladur walked with Tald to the town hall to ensure that he didn't have any problems getting into the room.

"I'll come by in the morning? We can walk down to the lake together. Beat the others down there, take a look around. Maybe we can even prepare a bit and get a leg up over the others." Caladur offered the idea as the men entered the town hall.

"Sounds great."

Caladur led Tald to the room and let him in. The two men shared a wish for a good night and parted ways. Tald fell asleep as soon as his body made contact with the mattress and Caladur left the town hall. He walked to the outside of the city and found an open field of grass where he laid down and took in the enormous expanse of the starry sky.

-18-

The morning light arrived, and Caladur took off with Tald to Lake Oznet. Many of the champions were still resting, but the pair agreed to get an early start that morning the night before. The walk to the lake was rather pleasant. Tald had gotten past his initial thoughts of Caladur's species and opened up to the elf.

"I'm just looking for a change," Tald began explaining his reasons for throwing his hat into the ring for becoming Rundor's next apprentice. "Rundor isn't my favorite champion, not by a long shot, but I can't deny the fact that he's the best. If I was able to get out of my dad's shop," the man paused for a moment, "for anything. I'd jump at it."

"Don't like working with your dad?"

"It's not that I don't like it, I just want to do something for myself. You know? And this is my shot. Even if I don't win this thing, I've learned a lot. I think I can at least open another shop in the city. My dad doesn't really want to expand. He thinks that it'll make the shop lose its character. I don't know. If I don't win this thing I might just go open my own shop. Clothing is getting boring. I mean, I'm twenty seven years old and have been selling clothes to the people of Fatiil since I was twelve. I'm getting sick of it. I might branch off and try something new. Something unique. I just don't know what yet. Any ideas?"

"Don't go planning that stuff yet. You're still in this. You're in the top fifty. We're both on our way Tald."

Tald smiled. "We're on our way. You and I Caladur. So, why are you trying out?"

The elf thought for a moment before he responded. He knew that this question was inevitable. He had been trying to formulate a response to the question all morning. "I've been an outcast my whole life. I've been living in the slums and saw this as an opportunity to provide for myself. An opportunity to bring a positive change for once." Caladur crafted the words with care. He didn't want to lie, but he wasn't ready to tell the whole story to this man he had only met the day before. The men were quiet while Caladur justified his statement within his mind and Tald awaited an explanation. Caladur thought to himself that he was an outcast his whole life. After all, he did realize that he was masquerading as something he wasn't for his entire life. The elf was satisfied with his justification and realized that Tald was waiting for more. "So what kind of clothes does your father's shop specialize in?"

"The high end stuff. Not too interesting. It's soft, it's tailored individually, and it's sold for a heck of a lot more than it's really worth."

The men stopped walking once they reached the shore of the lake.

"Like I said, I'm sick of it and I think I'm done working with clothes. I'd much rather just be a champion. Sure there's a risk, but I'd be a hero. My children would look *up* to me for a change." He laughed at his own short joke. "I'd bet that living the life of a champion is pretty nice too. The fame, the money, everything about it is appealing. At least to me."

"Yeah. Me too." Caladur agreed.

The pair looked over Lake Oznet in the midmorning. The surface of the enormous lake was as still as glass that reflected the green landscape and the pleasantly cloudy, blue sky. Throughout the part of the lake that came nearby the path from Ashwillow stood forty-five poles. Each was painted green.

Caladur and Tald were the first two participants to arrive at the lake and took a seat on the shore to eat a small breakfast they had packed earlier that morning. The men postulated about what the challenge of the day might be as they gazed across the expanse of Lake Oznet.

Gradually, more and more men arrived at the lake. About an hour before midday arrived, Yost came galloping down the path on his horse which he tied to a tree, giving the horse a bit of shade from the beaming sun. The sun had made its way to the middle of the sky by the time Rundor and the champion from the green shrine arrived at the lake.

"Welcome participants," Rundor proclaimed as he entered the area where most of the men gathered. "Today will once again separate the true participants from those who are only hopeful. As you have no doubt already seen, there are forty-five posts out there in the water. You will each swim out to one of the posts and mount it. If you are physically unable to climb to the top and balance yourself within a reasonable amount of time, you will be dismissed from the tryouts. I've not set a number on how many will continue after today, rather, a time limit. You must balance upon the post and remain standing there as long as you can. As soon as a part of your body hits the water, you'll be removed from the competition. Take a few moments to prepare yourself, then make your way out to the posts and take your place."

The thirty-five participants who were present began swimming out to the posts while the green champion and Rundor shared a few words. After their discussion, the green champion made his way into the water where he mounted one of the vacant posts.

Each post had a flat top that had a radius of about eight inches. The top of the wooden platform rose about three feet above the water and stood close to fifteen feet away from each other post. Caladur wrapped his arms around the wet, wooden pole and tried to pull himself to the top. After a bit of struggling with the smooth wood, his butt found the top of the pole. He took a moment to catch his breath before he made his way to his feet. Five other competitors, including Tald had already found their feet. The other men were struggling to make their way from the once calm water onto the pole. The men struggled with all of their might for another ten minutes. In the end, thirty-one men stood upon their posts, four failed to mount theirs before Rundor called an end to the preparation period.

"As you see, my fellow champion has opted to join you in this challenge. Everyone who remains dry at sundown will proceed to the next challenge. As an additional incentive, anyone who beats my comrade in this challenge will receive special training from both of us tomorrow morning. I will come back later this afternoon to declare the winners. Remember, any inappropriate behavior in this challenge will not be accepted. Best of luck to you all and hang tight. Sundown will arrive sooner than you expect. Take in the splendid view of this majestic lake."

Rundor took his leave from the lake. The men, for the most part, stood in silence on their posts. The surface of each post was large enough for both of their feet. After a couple hours, the discomfort of standing motionless for such a long time began to set in. The time passed slowly. Three hours after the competition began, one man fell off of his post while readjusting to sooth his discomfort. A long string of explicatives erupted from the man's mouth as he swam towards the shore. Two hours passed and two more men fell. Twenty-nine men remained standing, twenty-eight participants and one champion. Caladur judged that the sun had four more hours or so in the sky before it fell behind the horizon line.

About thirty minutes after the first group of men fell into the water, one of the remaining hopefuls steadied his balance, crouched down, and sat upon his pole. Caladur saw the stunt and thought that he would be able to make the shift to a sitting posture without falling off. Just before he began to move, the green champion called out to the sitting man.

"You're out."

"Me?" the man questioned.

"You're out." The green champion repeated.

"But they didn't say anything about,"

"You're out."

The man remained on his post for about twenty minutes in disbelief before he allowed himself to slip into the water, swim to the shore, and saunter back to the town of Ashwillow.

One hour of sunlight was left as the sun continued lowering in the evening sky. In the final hour, men began dropping one right after the next. Standing in one place with little to no chance for movement took a toll on a man's body. A larger toll than one would think. At last, the champion, who had not appeared to move a single inch throughout the entire day turned around on his post so he was facing the sunset in the west, turning his back on the competitors.

Rundor came back to the lake to find only eight contestants left standing alongside his fellow champion. Caladur refocused on his task as he observed the sun begin to disappear behind the darkening landscape. Only a few more minutes until he made his way to the next round of tryouts. The sun now was engulfed by the dark landscape, and Rundor called an end to the competition.

"Congratulations. You eight men have completed the third task of the series. You are now faced with a choice. You may choose to exit the competition now and make your way back to Ashwillow where you will be staying in the same room you had last night. Or, you may choose to continue in this challenge. If you remain in this challenge, you will be directly competing against a full-fledged champion of the Fatiilian Arena. If some miracle occurs and you win, you will be given transportation back to Fatiil with both of us and have the full journey to ask either of us anything. We will even provide some combat training tomorrow night. The choice is yours."

Yost was the first man into the water, followed by three other men just an instant after. Caladur thought for a moment before jumping off of this post and refreshing his tired body with the cool lake water.

Three men, including Tald remained on their poles. "I'm giving it a shot Caladur. I'll see you back in Fatiil." "Good luck Tald. We'll see you." Caladur called back after he swam out of the water and began on his way to the town of Ashwillow.

Halfway back to the town, Caladur spotted Yost waiting for him on the side of the road.

"Didn't feel like getting some extra training?" Yost's happy and inviting voice surprised Caladur. "Honestly, I was hoping you all tried to stay on those poles through the night. Tire yourselves out and give me an edge in the next challenge. I mean, think about it. Not a single one of us will outlast a champion. There's no way."

Caladur simply nodded in agreement. He didn't know what Yost's intentions were, but his opportunity for friendship was gone after he assaulted Caladur in the race around Fatiil, and further exiled by his confession of murder.

"C'mon. Don't you got anything to say tonight?"

Caladur tried to ignore the human. He failed. "You know, it's a great night. I think I'll just camp out here tonight." Caladur went off to the side of the path and took a deep breath. "You should stay too. Or do you need time to plan out how to cheat on the next trial?"

"Really? You can't even give me a little credit? I already know what I'm doing for the next trial. C'mon Caladur. You should know by now that my tactics are all planned. It's all calculated, and it's perfect. I'll never get caught. Will I? Anyway, I'd stay and chat with you a bit more, but I'm sure those girls are waiting to hear of my most recent victory. See you around Caladur." The words slithered out past Yost's snarled teeth and chilled Caladur's elven ears.

-19-

Caladur's exhausted body was lying in the same open field he had stayed in the night before. Clouds covered most of the sky and the shining stars behind them could not be seen. The adrenaline surge he had received after winning another challenge was beginning to wear off. He thought to return to his room in the town hall but, decided against it. Tald might use the room as soon as he fell off of his post. The elf went into his trance.

About four hours later, the cool night air began to chill the elf. His serene mind was unable to focus on anything but the cold air that surrounded his body. The young elf stood up, brushed himself off, and decided that he might as well begin his journey home. The thought of seeing Estine, Lucas and Celeste filled his head. He got his bearings and began walking towards the north.

Once the elf began moving, his body warmed and the cold was, for the most part, unnoticeable. Just before the sun began to rise, the clouds began to clear from the sky revealing the stars once more. The elf had made some good time through the night and was well on his way back to Fatiil. When the sun rose, he forced himself to stop and grab a bite to eat. The bread he had brought with him on his trip was beginning to get stale but it was something his new life had forced him to become accustomed to.

Later in the day, as the terrain began to flatten out once more, Yost caught up with him. The blonde haired man dismounted the horse and began walking aside Caladur. "You've made some pretty good time Caladur. It must be nice to not have the need to sleep each night."

The elf had no choice but to listen to the human.

"You don't talk much do you? Anyway, I figured I'd give my horse a break for a while. It's just plain luck that you happened to be on the road right when I was about to stop."

The two men continued walking.

"So I figured out what your advantage is."

"And?" The elf replied. He wasn't amused.

"You're an elf. A full blood elf. A member of the superior race, or so you think. You elves are all the same, frail, weak, pretty little people who walk through their unnaturally long lives without a care. That is, as long as a human never touches your flesh. You don't even need to try in these tasks do you? You just let your friends take care of everything while you just sit around and glide onward until you are given the title of apprentice.

"I must say," Yost continued after realizing that Caladur wasn't responding to his words, "you really went the whole nine yards with this charade. Pretending to be kicked out of the Order, living in the slums, it's all perfect. And now here you are in the top eight. So tell me, as a fellow deceiver, how are you pulling it off? How did you keep in the top one hundred in that race? I must have knocked you out for at least an hour."

Caladur paused. He didn't want to respond to the man, but his mouth began ranting. "I stayed in because I ran back to the purple champion's shrine, she recognized me and gave me another necklace which I used to get the stone from the guard. Then, in the next challenge I won because I managed to get enough points and remember my score. Yesterday, I advanced again due to my ability to stand on a pole in the middle of a lake for way too long. I am no longer a member of the Royal Order of True Elves, I live in the slums, and now, I'm going to become Rundor's apprentice. Not due to my connections. Not due to my blood. Not due to my dishonorable actions. But due to my natural abilities and my want, no, my need to beat you." The elf began walking again.

"Fine," Yost said, standing still. "Don't tell me. Keep up the farce." Caladur was distancing himself from the human. Yost shouted so he could be heard. "Your secret's safe with me buddy. Just like mine are with you." Yost got back on the stolen horse and urged the steed to a gallop, kicking up dirt on the elf as he rode onward towards Fatiil.

-20-

"Caladur!" Lucas shouted as he ran towards the elf who was becoming a big brother to him and jumped up to grapple his arms and legs around the elf's waist. "Did you win?"

"Not yet Lucas. But I'm still in it. I need to get back to the arena tomorrow to find out what the next challenge is. There are only eight of us left." He set the young boy back down on the street before he entered the small home in the slums of Fatiil. "I'm getting close," he said more to himself than to Lucas.

Inside, Estine and her daughter were playing with the now dirty rag doll Caladur had given her before he left. "Welcome back," Estine greeted the elf, "how did everything go?"

"Great. I made it to the next level. I've got today off before I need to be back to compete again. There's only eight of us left."

"Top eight? That's great Caladur. That means you'll be fighting in front of the public soon. Right?"

The thought had not occurred to Caladur. He knew he would be fighting for the public if he won, but the idea of doing that as a participant hadn't crossed his mind. "I don't know. I guess we'll be doing that soon. I'll be sure to let you know."

"We can't wait to watch you. Are you still up for dinner at my sister's tonight?"

"Yeah!" both of the young children shouted at once, oblivious to the fact that Estine was not asking them.

"Sure," Caladur laughed as he took a seat on the floor of the shack.

"Great. They'll expect us at sundown. We'll leave you to rest. It looks like you've had quite the journey."

"Thanks."

Later that evening, Estine and her children came to collect Caladur from the shack. They had each washed up and cleaned their clothes. The stains on their shirts were, at least to some extent, removed, but the holes remained. It seemed impossible to Caladur that their somewhat cleaned ensemble could make them as happy as it appeared to.

They began walking through the city. As they entered the housing district composed of the working class, Caladur became aware of unfavorable looks he received from many of the people. He felt like he was being hauled off to prison again, it was after all, the same street he was paraded down on his way to the jail.

After a short while, the family arrived at Estine's sister's home. Caladur recognized it from somewhere, but wasn't able to place it. He had only been through this part of the city a few times in his life and had never been to the particular home before. He followed behind Estine as she entered the short walk that approached the door of a modest home. It was two stories tall, but not very wide. Many of the homes within the city appeared this way. They weren't large, but had enough room for a family of four or five to live in comfort.

Estine knocked on the door and was greeted after a short while by a young woman. Caladur placed his memory of the home the instant he saw the girl's beautiful face. She was the beautiful human girl that caught Caladur's eye as the guard continued pulling him towards the prison. He couldn't be sure, but he thought that her eyes lit up as she remembered him too.

The young children, Celeste in particular, began hugging the beautiful, human girl shouting, "Lara! Lara!" over and over again.

"Hey guys," she welcomed the children into the home, "Dinner's almost ready. Go on and say hi to your aunt. Uncle G. should be home any time now."

The children were eager to enter the home and sit on the soft furniture, a luxury they infrequently had access to.

"Hi," Caladur broke the silence at the front door as he offered his hand, "I'm Caladur Vandel. And you are?"

"Lara. I've heard so much about you," she replied. Her soft hand was held firm by Caladur's as they shared a greeting that continued until it was awkward.

"I'll be inside. You two get to know each other." Estine excused herself, winking at Lara as she entered the home.

"So you're trying to become a champion? That's a pretty prestigious position in the city. Do you really think you'll make it all the way from a criminal to a position of honor so quickly?" Although her words were harsh, her voice was pleasant.

"I'm in the final eight. And plan to be number one. I can see most of the men are growing weary. The challenges are wearing them down. But I still feel strong."

"Feeling strong doesn't change the fact that you went to jail. What was that all about? Who is my family inviting into our home?" Her tone bit cold.

"It was a misunderstanding. My mother abandoned me, and I was in the home when the buyers came in. They had me hauled off to prison where I was held for a week."

"That's it?" she seemed skeptical.

"I didn't do anything wrong." He was sincere.

Lara gave the elf a doubtful glance.

Caladur was caught off of his guard. The way her eyes gazed at him seemed to pierce his soul. He tried to stutter out a response. "I, I, well, there's more to the story. But it'll take a while to explain," he regained his composure. "Maybe tomorrow evening I can take you out on a walk to tell you the whole story."

She smiled.

"For now, I smell delicious food, and I don't think we should keep it, I mean your family, waiting."

Caladur and Lara entered the home to find the children, Estine, and Estine's sister sitting in the well furnished living room.

Dinner consisted of delicious chicken prepared by Estine's sister. The flavor of the poultry enveloped Caladur's taste buds as he slowly chewed his body's nourishment. The taste of the bird was comparable to the food Caladur ate while he was a part of the Order. The nourishment he consumed with the coins he obtained from begging was bad. The food the arena provided him was better, but only by a small margin. The chicken that Caladur was sharing with his new friends put everything he had eaten over the past week to shame.

The dinner stretched late into the evening. Everyone had their own questions of Caladur's experience in the tryouts for the apprenticeship. Lucas and Celeste were preoccupied with questions about what or who he was forced to fight. They were let down every time he explained that he had not been in direct combat with anyone else. He took care to skip over his interactions with Yost. Estine and her sister asked all about the other participants. What they were like. Caladur told them mostly about Tald. He also told them of the overreactions from most of the participants who were cut from the tryouts. Uncle G. asked about the details of each challenge, comparing his personal abilities to those of the participants.

"So how are you able to overcome these challenges?"

Caladur answered with a confused glance.

"I mean, how were you able to run for so long? Keep in the challenge after you got hit on the head with a metal ball? Stand on a pole for hours? Deal with being forced to just leave on a week-long journey at a moment's notice? I just don't think I'd be able to do it."

"It's been tough. I've always been a good runner. It calms me down so I when I was younger, I would just go on a run. I guess that prepared me for the challenge. As for getting hit with the ball. It was right at the end of the event. Had it occurred at the beginning, I would have been kicked out of the competition." He took a bite of the warm roll he had saved for last. "As for standing on a pole for six plus hours, it sucked. But that's done now and I likely won't ever have to do something like that again. And leaving at a moment's notice? It's not too bad. I don't have much going on otherwise. No family or commitments are really holding me here. So I actually enjoyed that opportunity. Believe it or not, I hadn't been outside of the city before then."

"It's amazing," Lara replied. "Everything you've been through and to think you still have more ahead of you before you win. I guess they need to make it pretty brutal if they want the right apprentice. Especially for Rundor."

"Guess so," Caladur agreed.

After the dinner, which lasted well over two hours, Estine, her children, and Caladur took leave from the home. Everyone shared goodbyes. Caladur was pleased to find that he was well-liked by the entire family. He shared handshakes with Uncle G. and his wife as they wished him luck. Lara confirmed that he would come by the next night to escort her around the city to which he agreed.

The family Caladur had found himself becoming a part of made their way back to the shack in the slums they called home a short while later. The children laid down to sleep. The excitement of the evening sapped their energy. Estine watched over them as she allowed herself to be lulled to sleep bit by bit. Then, Caladur entered his trance. It was unusual. He wasn't able to get his mind off of Lara. Her beautiful dark brown hair looked to be so soft. Her brown eyes encircled by dark eyelashes. Her inviting lips that Caladur restrained himself from exploring, which proved to be the most difficult task he had to face since being removed from the elven society.

-21-

In the morning, Caladur resumed his work at *Sutur's This's and That's*. Without Caladur's watchful eye for a week, the shop was beginning to sit in disarray again. He spent an hour tidying up the front before he resumed his work in the back. The work went slow. It may have been the fact that the work was uneventful, but Caladur felt that the persistent questioning from Mr. Sutur regarding the details of his latest challenge and the journey to Ashwillow contributed. It wasn't that he was annoyed by the man, he, in fact, had come to respect him from the time they spent working together, but he was growing tired of all the attention that came with being involved with the arena.

"Why didn't you try to beat the champion? I'm sure an elf like you would have been able to stay on the post longer than any human." Mr. Sutur sat on a stool sipping from a cup of tea while he supervised Caladur working.

The elf set down the crate he was moving. "I wanted to keep my energy for the next event. I was about to fall anyway. The patience it takes to stand still for hours on end was just about unbearable." He began moving another crate.

Crash.

The sound came from the front of the store. Caladur beat Mr. Sutur out of the back room and into the shop where he found a large stone sitting amongst shattered glass on the floor of the store. The entire front window had been shattered. Caladur surveyed the mess for a moment before he spotted Oranton within the small crowd of onlookers.

"Oranton!" he called, but his old friend simply turned his back and began walking down the morning streets of Fatiil.

"Was that him?" Mr. Sutur asked. "Was he the elf who did this?"

Caladur had never seen anything but a smile on the man's face, even when he first met him and the older man was struggling with a crate. But now, his expression was different. It was anger. But there was more. An expression of confusion surfaced.

"Yeah. I can just about guarantee he was the one."

Mr. Sutur just stood there in disbelief, gazing upon the broken glass. "Do you know how expensive that was?"

"I'm sorry." The young elf couldn't help but think that the attack was his fault.

"Sorry?" the old man's smile was back. "You did nothing wrong. It's the other elves. They feel that they have some sort of right to be disrespectful of everyone else. I don't know why they get that. It's just something we've got to live with I guess." He began walking to the back room again. "I'll get a broom to clean it up. Feel free to take off to the arena. I know it's about that time." Mr. Sutur, at a slow pace, made his way to the back room to retrieve a pan and broom. Yet, to his surprise, when he returned, Caladur was still waiting for him in the front room.

"I'll take care of it. Go enjoy your tea. You've got plenty work to take care of after I leave." He gave Mr. Sutur a smile as the elf took the broom and dustpan from his employer.

-22-

"Congratulations. You eight men have overcome thousands of others to make it to this point. For that I commend you. Each of you has proven yourselves in many different ways. You've managed to pass the test of dexterity. Recently, you've passed the test of endurance. Today, your strength, and your wisdom, will be tested. Unlike the last challenges, this challenge will be team based. Only four of you will move on.

"You will have one hour to form two teams. By the end of this period, you, and your three team members, must each accept everyone else on your team. The trial will test your team's physical strength against the other. The winning team will move onto the next round. The losers will be dismissed from this tournament.

"As you can see, the ranks are thinning. While choosing your team, think carefully. The people on your team will be moving on with you, so you will want to be sure that you fully believe you can best each of them. However, only the stronger team will move on. I'll be back in an hour. Think thoroughly, decide carefully. See you soon."

Tald and Caladur met eyes without delay. Despite his small stature, Caladur knew that he possessed a good amount of strength. Three other men united without a thought. They had been attached at the hip throughout each of the trials. While they conversed during this time, Caladur gathered that they were brothers. A fourth had been in the tryouts, but was dismissed after the dexterity competition at the Fatiilian Rings. One of the remaining three men hurriedly made his way to the brothers. He was not the most built man in the room, that would be the youngest of the brothers, but he was still accepted. The groups had been decided, with little input from anyone but the brothers. Caladur was matched with Tald, a man who appeared to have a least a little bit of elven blood in him, and, to his disgust, Yost.

The two teams separated to different sides of the room to discuss the upcoming event with their teammates. Yost was the first to begin speaking, "Looks like you'll be helping me advance once more Caladur. You've helped me out so much already. Are you sure you can do it again?"

Tald and the other participant, Mitlo, appeared to be confused by the coded comment. Tald pressed on and began addressing the group in a quiet voice. "Alright, I know what the challenge is. On the way back to Fatiil, during my training,"

"You won?" Caladur blurted out.

"I was the last standing. The champion could have gone on, but after the other participants fell, he simply jumped off, awarding me the training. But that doesn't matter. What does is that they told me what the challenge was. To give me, and I guess us all, a little edge over the others. And based on the way the teams worked out, we'll need it. Their team is likely the stronger of the two, but we're past that now. The challenge is an obstacle course divided into four segments. Each of us will take one. First team to finish the race wins.

"Now, I got the first leg no question. Cal here should bring up the tail. As for the middle, I guess whoever is faster should take the third leg."

Mitlo raised his hand. "I'd be the fastest." Tald didn't let Yost disagree and accepted the statement.

"So Yost, that puts you on the second leg."

Everyone but Yost nodded, eager to get the next challenge started. "Care to tell me what the legs consist of so that we can form order as a team?"

"We'll be fine with this order. We all just need to give it our all and we can make it to the semi-finals." Tald explained.

Yost quickly left the group, and he made his way to the others. He was shooed away at first, but a moment later, after they finished their speculations on the unknown event, they allowed him to converse.

"So what was the training like?" Caladur asked his friend as they awaited Rundor's return.

"Nothing too fantastic. The best thing they did for me was give me a ride home. The carriage trip was faster than walking, and the rest was needed. I stood on that pole until a few hours before sunup. Obviously, they also gave me a rather large pointer about this challenge."

"What about the next round?" Mitlo asked with a hope for information.

"No, just this one. If they gave me more it would be too unfair. Don't you think? Anyway, they offered a few pointers on what life is like after becoming a champion. The fame, the constant cheering, the pressure of living a public life, you know, the downside that most people don't see or even think about."

Caladur and Mitlo spoke to Tald a short while longer while he told of his journey home with the champions.

In due course, Rundor came back into the room. "Alright. Let's get moving. Time to test your team's strength. The men followed Rundor through the bowels of the Fatiilian Arena until they came to a set of stairs. "The arena is right up these steps. It's empty now, but you'll get a feel of fighting in front of the population soon enough. That is, if you win this competition."

The men entered the arena which had been completely made over. Everyone but Caladur realized this immediately. Instead of a large, open oval, the arena was cluttered with large wooden obstacles.

They were each directed to their individual starting line where they awaited the start of the competition. Rundor boomed, "First team to complete the course advances to the semi-finals. On your marks, get set," he looked from Tald to eldest of the brothers, Oryt, "Go!"

The relay began and Tald accelerated to a sprint, just behind his adversary. Once he reached the wire, he dropped to his chest without hesitation and began crawling through the mud pit ensuring that his back didn't get caught on the barbed wire hanging only an inch above. The tunnel felt much longer than it appeared to be when outside of it.

Inch by inch he created a gap between himself and the other competitor. The end was drawing near, he sped up, giving the task every ounce of energy his small body held. As soon as his head was out from underneath the obstacle, he pushed himself up to his feet, but the wiring latched into his shirt and skin. He screamed, more from surprise than from pain and struggled to dethatch his shirt from the barbs.

Yost, who was the second man on Caladur's team, began shouting at Tald in fury. The other team's second runner, Danxale, had begun the next leg while Tald was trying to untangle his shirt from the barbs. Finally, in a fit of rage, Tald slipped backwards out of the tattered shirt and then completed the event by tagging Yost's hand.

Yost was way behind, but sprinted on regardless. He leaped onto the netting, giving the unstable contraption a shake which caused the adversary to lose footing on the webbed rope. Yost then took his time to climb the gentle incline of rope, ensuring that his feet found purchase with each step.

Although his entrance to the course caused his opponent to stumble, the opponent reached the platform before Yost was even a quarter of the way up. Yost pressed on. The obstacle was much easier when he was the only person on the rope lattice.

He found his way to the top where he simply disregarded the ladder and jumped ten feet to the dusty dirt below. He landed in a roll and quickly tagged Mitlo, the third runner of Caladur's team. Yost closed a bit of the gap but there was still much to gain.

Mitlo sprinted one lap around the outside of the arena, slightly closing the enormous gap, step by step. Once his lap was complete, he came to his pit. Within the pit hissed a large viper, ready to strike anyone who captivated its attention. Mitlo didn't waste a moment. He grabbed a sword from the ground and jumped into the pit. He saw one of the brother's, Angen, acting timid around the snake in a neighboring pit and knew he could pick up some ground for his team.

Once inside, he focused his concentration on the angered wild animal. He prepared a strike but his approach was interrupted by a vicious attack from the venomous serpent. Mitlo dodged but needed to resituate his attack. As soon as he was ready, he brought the sword around in one swift and powerful attack, severing the top quarter of the body from the rest.

When the body quit moving, Mitlo jumped out of the pit and sprinted towards Caladur. The youngest brother, Tiany, had already been tagged and started up the rope, but Caladur was tagged only a few seconds later.

The young elf jumped up and grabbed the rope. With all of his might, he pulled his body weight up from knot to knot. Yet despite his best effort, his adversary was getting further and further ahead. Caladur climbed on, hoping that the youngest brother would slow down, but that didn't seem to be happening.

Caladur had about fifteen feet of the thirty foot climb complete when an opportunity opened. The youngest brother was only five feet from the top when his left hand slipped from the rope. He struggled to hang on with his right but was unable to get another grip with his left. Caladur climbed further and faster, not letting the opportunity slip past him.

Caladur made his way to be even with the struggling man.

"Help!" he said in a gasp.

Caladur could see that the man was clearly in pain and in danger of falling twenty-five feet to the hard ground below.

"Hold on," Caladur said while climbing, "I'll pull you up."

The man nodded, but Caladur could tell that his ability to hold on was vanishing rapidly.

A few seconds later, Caladur found the safety of the high wooden platform. He couldn't reach the man, but he began pulling the rope in an effort to save him. It was too heavy. He tried again and was able to pull up an inch or so.

"Help!" Caladur called to the men below, but they were already on their way. The other brothers were the first to arrive up the wooden planks that connected the platform to the safety of the ground.

Caladur let the brothers get through so they could try to pull their brother up. They struggled to pull the rope up about a foot, allowing enough room for Caladur to grab onto the rope and help pull the struggling man up to safety.

Angen began counting. "One. Two. Three!"

They pulled him up another foot. Three to go.

"One. Two. Three!"

The men pulled once more with a mighty force to save the endangered competitor. However, the jerk in the rope caused Tiany to lose his grip. He crashed down to the ground. A series of snaps resounded as his legs collapsed in unnatural ways under the force of his body. Consciousness left him.

Rundor arrived at the sleeping man with everyone else. He was alive, but his legs were shattered. Rundor summoned the arena's doctors while the competitors stood around silently.

Rundor, while working with the injured competitor, announced Caladur's team as the winners and then focused entirely on bringing Tiany back to consciousness. Caladur was the last of his team to leave the arena. He surveyed the stands which could hold thousands of people at any time. He did his best to think about how he would be able to manage conducting himself in battle in front of so many onlookers. His stomach churned slightly before he made his way back through the arena's passages and to the streets.

"You're welcome," Yost said after appearing from within the crowds of people.

Caladur ignored the human he had come to despise.

"I said you're welcome." A pause. "Do you think we could have really beaten those brothers without some help?"

Caladur walked on. He didn't want to know what the man did, but he heard anyway.

"First of all, I already knew it was a team competition. It's amazing what you can learn for a few gold pieces. Anyway, I met up with the brothers the other night at the Rusty Mace, over on the west side for a few drinks. I wasn't going to help them get to the end, they would crush me if I had to fight them. So I decided to team up with y'all. After all, I know I can best you in personal combat. But I played nice with them. Bought them a few drinks, they bought me a few. It was a good night, they're good people. Almost as good as you. Oh, excuse me ma'am." Yost, in his telling of the story, wasn't watching where he was going and almost ran over a young girl. "Anyway, I put some of this elixir in that strong one's drink. I bought it a few months ago, thought it would come in handy. It did. See, it causes cramps whenever physical exertion occurs within the next couple days. Quite a powerful little drug. Then, I turned off the charm, made them hate me, so I knew I wouldn't be on their team, and left. Now we're in the semi-finals. You're welcome."

Throughout the monologue, Caladur had picked up his pace, made frantic turns, slowed down, pulled a one-eighty, but the human stayed in step with the elf, devoted to sharing the story.

"Of course, now, you're party to this misbehavior. You know about it. You've benefited from it. Do you still think I'm such a bad guy? I got you to the semi-finals."

A fuse blew in Caladur. He turned to the man and shoved him to the ground.

Yost only began laughing. "There's the spirit."

"Stay out of my business. I'll win this competition on my own. I don't need your help. I'll see you tomorrow for the next round. I just hope that I'll be able to fight you again. To show you what I can really do." Caladur kicked some dirt from the ground onto of Yost, who was still chuckling to himself before the elf made his way back to the slums.

-23-

Caladur knocked on the door that stood before him. The evening sun was turning the sky orange. There was about an hour of sunlight left in the city's sky. He had just rested for a few hours in the slums, but now it was time to keep another commitment. This one, he had been looking forward to all day.

Uncle G. opened the door and gave Caladur a stern look. "I understand you are going to be taking my daughter on a walk this evening." The jolly aura that surrounded the man the night before was not there. "You do understand that she's a good girl. Not the typical type you arena men hang around. Right?"

"Yes sir." Caladur muttered the words with as much gusto as he could manage.

Uncle G. sighed. "You're lucky Estine vouched for you. Don't make me regret this and don't keep her out too late."

"Yes sir." A little more convincing this time.

"Lara," Uncle G. called back into his home. "Caladur's here for you."

There was no pause. She was already descending the stairs by the time he finished saying her name. It was apparent that she had prepared for the walk. Her clothes appeared to be new, her hair was set in a perfect manner. The left-hand portion of her bangs was held behind her round ear while the right-side portion of her soft hair dangled playfully in front of her face. The dark hair contrasted with her tan skin. The look was very pleasing to Caladur's eyes.

"Hi," he mumbled.

"Hi," she chirped with an eager voice. "Let's go. It's already getting late." She grabbed his hand and led him away from the home.

The elf didn't have enough time to realize what had just happened before he was walking down the busy city streets holding the girl's warm hand.

"So, you promised to tell me the whole story." She didn't waste any time getting to the point.

"Where do you want me to start?" he asked. The jitters of the night had left. He felt comfortable. Completely at peace. Even though he had not told everyone about his excommunication yet, he did not harbor any reservations against sharing with Lara. "My father left my mother and me while I was young. I don't remember him at all.

"That must have been hard," Lara interrupted.

"Trust me, it gets worse than that. Much worse. Anyway, I was brought up as an elf within the Royal Order of True Elves. That was my life. I only associated with other elves, I committed some deeds against non-elves that I probably shouldn't have. Nothing I did was too serious, but I'm not proud of any of that stuff. I guess I used to be, but I've changed so much since then. It seems like forever ago now. So, my mother ran out of money and had requested to receive some from the ROTE. That was what we would call the Order." Caladur explained. "The ROTE gave her the money, which she took, before telling anyone that she had sold the house. Then, she left. She took the money from the ROTE and from the home, and she left the city, refusing to take me with her."

The ease of the telling of the story amazed Caladur. He suspected that the comfort of Lara holding his hand may have helped. He felt no emotion for the ROTE. He didn't miss anything about it. He believed he was happy with his life. "Well, I spent one final night in the home. I expected the people to move in later that afternoon. I was wrong. They came to the home in the early morning and found me inside. I tried to leave without cause, but the man who bought the house pinned me while his wife got the guard.

"I sat in prison for a week. Coming to grips with my new life. I didn't know where I would go. I didn't know what I would do. I didn't even know what I would be able to find to eat. I only got out because a man named Owsin told his son to buy my bail instead of his own. That was the first gift I was given by a human. Without that, I don't know if I would have been able to survive outside of the jail. The night after I got out, I met Estine and her children. They were nice enough to give me housing until I got my feet back under me. I begged for money for a while, just enough to buy some food. Now, the arena provides me with enough food. I was lucky enough to find a job working for a man, Mr. Sutur, to keep me busy. I clean his shop and keep things in order for him. But you saw all that the other day. It doesn't pay much, and it doesn't pay frequently. I've actually only been paid once. But it's been enough to keep me alive and the job gives me something to do. Mr. Sutur's one of the nicest men I've ever met. You'll need to officially meet him sometime.

"Anyway, I heard of the opportunity at the arena and jumped at it. Reluctantly at first, but now I'm so close. I can almost taste it. There's only three people between me and Rundor. If I get this, I'll be back on top. I'll have something again."

Caladur proceeded to tell Lara about Yost. About the different ways he has cheated in order to stay in the competition.

"You should tell someone," Lara urged him.

"I can't. Now I've benefited from his tactics. I'm just going to beat him. Ensure that he doesn't become the apprentice. The best way I know how to do it now is by winning this."

Lara didn't answer, but it was clear to Caladur that she was disappointed in his decision.

"So what about you?" Caladur tried to change the subject to something else. "Now that you know everything about me, tell me about yourself."

Lara turned down the next street and smiled. "I'm afraid that will need to wait. It's late and you promised my father." She pointed towards her home. "I guess we'll just have to do this again sometime."

They shared a smile as they continued walking to her home. The cool summer night was pleasant, and

Caladur's story made the time pass so fast it seemed impossible to the elf. "I had a great time."

"Me too," Lara squeezed the elf's hand as they locked eyes. "I'll see you soon."

"Yes you will." He brought her hand to his mouth to give the back a soft kiss. "Goodnight Lara."

"Goodnight Caladur. And good luck tomorrow." The girl disappeared into her home. As she closed the door, Caladur caught a glimpse from her father, staring him down through the cracked door. Just before the door closed, Uncle G. smiled.

-24-

The next morning couldn't have come too soon. Life seemed so bland to the elf when he was waiting in the shack for morning. The future was holding too many questions for him to enjoy the starry night sky. He tried to focus his mind on the questions surrounding the semifinals of the tournament, but he kept thinking about his night with Lara. The girl's face consumed his mind's eye. The phantom memory of the sound of her voice spoke the words he wished to hear from her.

Many times he shook his head to try to refocus on the task at hand, his competition for the chance to become Rundor's apprentice. His attempts, for the most part, failed. The night was long and full of daydreams of his next meeting with Lara.

At last, the sun began to rise and he began his day, just as he always did. He went to *Sutur's This's and That's.*

The store looked different. The large glass display window had been covered up with a large slab of wood, sheltering the inside of the store from the elements. Inside, the shelves had been reconstructed and set up. With the exception of the display window, there was no apparent difference to the store.

Mr. Sutur's joy had returned. Had Caladur not experienced the stone coming through the window the day before, he wouldn't have been able to detect any difference. He spent the morning rearranging the boxes for Mr. Sutur in the back while he drank his tea. The men talked about Caladur's feminine interests and about the trials from the previous day.

The time drifted by until Caladur began making his way to the arena to learn about the semi-finals. While entering the arena, he saw Tald. "Tald!" he called out over the crowd. The man didn't turn around, he must not have heard over the crowd.

Caladur entered the arena a few moments later, just behind Tald. "Tald!" he called again.

This time the short man turned around. "Hey, how's it going?"

"Pretty good. I wish I knew what we were going to be doing today. Any idea?" Caladur had a sense that Tald knew a little bit more than he let onto the other day in front of the other men.

He shook his head. "They only told me about the obstacle course. I'd tell you more if I knew."

Caladur thought he was telling the truth. "Well, whatever it is, best of luck to you. If I don't get it, I'd choose you over the others." He lowered his voice. "Honestly, if I don't get it, I don't care who does, as long as Yost doesn't. He doesn't deserve it."

"No?" Tald asked. "Why do you say that?"

"He's not been the most, upstanding competitor."

"What do you mean?"

"I shouldn't say."

"C'mon Caladur." Tald urged.

"Fine. If you really want to know, I can tell you later. But not here. We can grab dinner together later if you want."

"Sure." Tald smiled as they entered the training room. Mitlo was already inside the room. Yost joined them a few minutes later.

Once everyone was seated and settled, Rundor entered the room. This time, he was wearing a full suit of armor and was carrying a large sword. He appeared to be ready for battle. Each of the participants grew worried. Based on his ensemble, they thought it was time to meet Rundor in battle, something that each man feared.

"The final four," his voice was calm. "We've come to the time where the tryouts will become public. One week from today, you will display your talent as a champion in front of the people of Fatiil. One week from today, you will meet a fierce beast in combat within the arena. As I said at the beginning of this competition, your physical wellbeing is at risk. You will be fighting a wild animal that does not know restraint. Even though we will be watching out for you, and should you call for help, we will be there, the chance for death, or severe physical harm is present.

"Once again, I would like to extend to each of you an invitation to back out. No one will be looked down upon for valuing their lives outside of this competition over the chance to proceed further. You have this entire week to think about this. Please, drop out if you are not fully committed." Rundor paused to let the reality of their situation sink in.

"I will personally be judging the battles. Based on your performance, I will choose two finalists who will compete in one final test for the position of my apprentice. Remember, while you train this week, you will be judged on all aspects of a true Fatiilian champion. You must have the strength to fight, you must have the endurance to stay in the battle, you must have the nimbleness to dodge and make perfectly aimed attacks, you must have the wisdom to make life or death decisions in an instant, finally, you must be a performer. The public of Fatiil does not come to the arena to watch the champions slaughter animals. They come for a show. Make it good. Keep it lively."

The champion, covered in armor, took his leave from the room allowing the champions to process the new challenge. For Caladur, it wasn't the fact that he would be fighting in a life or death situation, it was that the crowd would be enormous. Thousands of people would be watching him engage an animal that would not stop until he was dead. The thought of the exposure frightened Caladur as he and Tald made their way out of the arena's bowels.

-25-

Caladur accompanied Tald to a small pub in the business district. It was late in the afternoon, but the men agreed to have an early dinner while they discussed their swiftly approaching debut in the arena. The pub was still pretty empty due to the early hour, and the men quickly found a small table that suited them.

The bar maiden approached the men to take their order. She appeared to be eager to have people in the pub so early. More customers meant a few more coins for her pocket.

The two men ordered a mug of ale. Caladur began ordering the cheapest cut of meat offered. "I'll take a chicken breast, well cooked please."

"Chicken?" Tald interrupted. "We're celebrating making it this far. You'll have a steak." He turned to the bar maiden. "Two of your finest steaks."

She turned to begin preparing the meat before Caladur could protest.

"Relax. It's on me. We've made it. We are fighting in the arena. The Fatiilian Arena. We are going to be known throughout the city. Even if we don't get the apprenticeship, we will have taken our first step to becoming a champion. Another champion may spot us and take us under his wing. We've done it Caladur." The joy around Tald was palpable.

The steak arrived and was consumed. The men savored each bit of seasoned beef in their mouth. "So, you were saying something about Yost earlier. What was that about?"

"He's been cheating at every step of the tourney. He didn't even run the preliminary race. Instead, he jumped me and stole my necklaces. He admitted to me that he poisoned one of the brothers in order to win the obstacle course, which he knew about by bribing some people within the arena. That's just a few of his credits."

Tald didn't seem to be surprised. "Good for him," he said like it was nothing.

"Excuse me?"

"Good for him," Tald repeated before clarifying. "If he's able to work the system well enough to consistently win these challenges and go undetected, he deserves to be here."

"You can't tell me," Caladur began before he was cut off.

"Listen. I don't think it's the best or most righteous way to participate. But if it's what serves him, then we can't judge him. Remember, they said our wisdom will be tested. Maybe that's what they meant. If he has the foresight and ability to covertly sabotage others in this tournament. Not to mention the will to go through with it after Rundor's warning. Why hold it against him?"

Caladur couldn't believe that the one man he found within the competition to be a friend was supporting the underhanded ways of the man who had almost ruined his chances from the very beginning. "He killed a man for his horse." He had omitted that bit during the first report. He didn't think he would need to say it in order to get Tald's attention.

"Well that is a bit much."

"A bit much?" Caladur raised his voice in the all but empty pub. "Taking another man's life in order to get a slight advantage in this tournament is 'a bit much'?" He didn't realize he was standing until he had finished speaking.

"Alright Caladur. Take a seat and think this through."

"No!" All sense had left him. His mind was in the same place it was when he lost control and beat the tar out of Oranton at the True Elf Rings in another life. "I won't sit down. I won't calm down. You're just as bad as him if you think he wasn't acting out of turn."

"Me?" Tald was now on his feet, although, his short stature didn't have the same effect as Caladur. "You're the one who knew about these transgressions throughout the tourney. Yet, you didn't turn him in. I'd even put money on the fact that I'm the first one within the tryouts who you've told." He was seething. "Am I right!?"

Caladur looked down upon the man for a moment before he turned his back and left the pub.

"You'll understand once you have a little more experience under your belt. Nothing is black and white. He's had reason. You don't know where he came from. I'd expect someone like you from the slums to understand that."

Tald continued shouting after Caladur, but after he left the restaurant, he was unable to hear the short human's words. The young elf quickly walked through the city. His mind wasn't sure of his destination, but his body seemed to know where it was going.

After a short while, he found himself knocking on Lara's door. The young girl quickly came to the door, opened it and greeted the elf with a smile.

"Hi. I guess if you insist, I'll go on another walk with you. I'll be right back." She retreated to the back room of the first floor for a moment. Before Caladur knew what happened, she returned. "My dad says same rules and same times apply. Also he says to have fun. Bye!" she called back into her home before closing the door and leading the surprised elf towards the streets. "Couldn't stay away from me for more than one day?"

The quickness of the situation caught up to Caladur at last. "Honestly?"

"Of course."

"I didn't realize I was coming to see you until I was at your door." He forced a laugh, hoping the girl wouldn't take offense to the comment. "I had a fight with another one of the competitors. I guess I just came to you because I knew you would listen."

She smiled. "What is it?"

Caladur told her of Tald's reaction to the news of Yost as they meandered through the city. After venting for a few moments, he remembered that she hadn't told him anything about her life yet. He'd been doing all of the talking since they met. "I'm sick of talking about it. How about you tell me something about yourself for a change?"

"Alright. What do you want to know?"

"Anything. Um. What do you do for fun?"

"Pass."

"Pass? You can't pass."

"But it's silly. You'll just laugh."

"C'mon," the elf prodded.

"Fine," she lowered he head as well as her voice, "I really enjoy going to the arena with my friends to watch the fights."

"What?" Caladur laughed out. "Why is that funny?"

"You're the one who's laughing."

"I'm only laughing at the fact that you thought that would make me laugh."

"You're making no sense. You do realize that right?" She laughed a bit to herself.

He stopped. "I'm sorry." He cleared this throat. "That's cool though." He thought about whether or not he should tell her about his chance to perform in the arena next week for a moment before deciding against it. "One of these days I'll probably be fighting there. You going to come watch me?"

"Of course."

He grabbed her hand as they continued walking through the streets.

"Anything else you do?"

"I like to paint. I'm not the best, but I enjoy it."

"So when are you going to paint me?" He did his best to sound sarcastic, but his mouth betrayed him and did a poor job of concealing his hope behind a shroud of derision.

"I'll paint you when you become a champion."

"Deal. But before I let you paint me, I'll need to see some of your other work. Just to be sure you're not absolutely horrible."

She broke away from his hand and gave him a stern look. "You think my work is horrible?"

"No." Her reaction took him by complete surprise. "I think it'll be,"

While he was trying to recover from the pit he dug himself into, Lara lunged at Caladur and begin tickling his sides. The elf quickly retaliated and learned that he could take a tickling better than she could. As soon as he found her weak spot, she lost control of her body and began cracking up and jumping around, trying to get away. After a short bit of torture, he released the girl who grabbed his hand as they continued walking.

Lara opened up to Caladur sharing many things about her life with the elf. Caladur learned that she had a younger brother who died to an illness three years ago and that she still had troubles letting the thoughts of him leave. She had a special place for her aunt Estine in her heart. She acted like an older sister through the hard times, in particular through the sickness and death of her younger brother. Her favorite color was deep green, just like summer grass. Her favorite season was autumn because the trees light on fire and become a beautiful work of art. She also confessed to going a few steps out of her way to stomp on an especially crunchy looking leaf.

The couple came upon *Sutur's This's and That's* along their walk rather inadvertently. As they passed by, Caladur insisted that they go inside and say hi to Mr. Sutur. "He has heard about you," Caladur admitted as they entered the store.

"Caladur! Welcome. What brings you by tonight?" The man was so excited to see his elven employee that he didn't notice the girl accompanying him at first. "Oh dear, I'm sorry. You must be Lara. Right? Caladur has told me so much about you. He said you were beautiful, but I had no idea how right he was. It's my pleasure to finally make your acquaintance."

Lara reached out and shook the hand of the eccentric man. "Caladur's told me about you too. He said you're the best boss a person could ask for."

"Did he now? He speaks too highly of me then. I always feel terribly when he's working so hard and all my body can do is supervise and drink my tea. But then, I guess if I were more capable, I wouldn't need him to be here and we'd have never met. But that's the way life works sometimes. Despite the terrible things, the pieces fall perfectly into place. Right?"

Lara and Caladur nodded in agreement, sharing a slight smile

"Well, is there anything I can get either of you?" the man offered.

"No. We were just stopping in to say hi. I need to get her back home before the sunlight is gone."

"Well don't let me keep you. I'll see you in the morning Caladur. And it was a pleasure to make your acquaintance Lara. Have a great night you two."

"Thanks, you too," Lara said while exiting the store. Once outside, she turned towards the wooden panel that had replaced the glass display window. "I miss that window. I loved looking into the store to see what crazy stuff might be inside."

"Yeah. It's a shame. The window was perfect for a store like his. Now it just looks like everything else. But I guess it's like he said. You take the bad as it comes and eventually, everything falls into place."

Lara agreed as the two walked hand in hand back to her home. A block or two away, they shared a brief hug before Caladur kissed the back of the girl's hand. Then they finished their walk home.

"Good night."

"Good night Caladur. I had a great time again. See you soon."

Caladur left the girl's home and blissfully strolled back to the slums where stayed for the night with Estine and her children.

-26-

Five days remained until he was to fight in the arena. He spent his first day of training working at *Sutur's This's and That's*. On the second morning, he arrived at the shop to a surprise. The large wooden slab covering the remains of the broken window had been decorated, or rather painted. The words "*Sutur's This's and That's*" were painted in large, green letters. The words formed an arch over another series of yellow words that said, "Your home for Fatiil's finest unique and unordinary items." The words were crisp and clean, whoever painted it took the care to do a great job. The rest of the panel was covered with various depictions of some of the more popular items sold in the store. He knew right away who painted the wood. Lara.

"Mr. Sutur," Caladur called as he entered the front room of the shop. "You want me to start by tidying the front?"

After hearing a "Yes" from the back, he began his work. It took little more than fifteen minutes to make the front look as good as new. Over the past weeks, he had become adept at recreating the newness of the shop every day. With his standing assignment complete, he entered the back room to join with Mr. Sutur in drinking a cup of tea before resuming his work in rearranging the crates of various odds and ends in the back. The day before, he completed a good deal of work. He thought if he worked just as hard again, he would be able to complete his project that day.

"What are you doing to train for the big day?" Mr. Sutur asked while they were drinking their tea.

"Moving crates," he said for a laugh. "I don't know. I'm going to the arena tonight with Lara. In honesty, I've never been inside the arena while it has been open."

Mr. Sutur almost spit out his tea. "You've never seen a fight in the arena and you're trying out? Don't you care to know what you're getting yourself into?"

"I didn't care what it was when I first signed up. I've had a few doubts come up since then. Especially since Lara came around, but I'm enjoying the competition and unless I'm completely appalled by the games tonight, I plan on seeing these tryouts through to the end."

"Good for you. Quitting never gets you anywhere."

"And you're living proof."

"I am?"

"Yeah. I know a lot of people would have given up or done something rash if someone trashed their shop. But you just put up some wood and painted it up to make it look even better than before."

"I guess I would be living proof then. But, I didn't do the painting. Someone came in the middle of the night and did it. I expected you, but I guess I was wrong. Either way. You're doing the right thing, sticking to your guns in the competition. If you dropped out, one of those cheats might get the spot."

Caladur finished his tea and resumed his work. By the late afternoon, he had successfully rearranged the back room to Mr. Sutur's standards. It would now be much easier to pick out a crate with which to restock the front with. All thanks to the elf who helped a struggling man lift a crate onto a cart for nothing in exchange.

On his way out of the shop, Mr. Sutur stopped the elf. "Thank you so much. You have no idea how much your work will help me. I truly appreciate everything you've done. Honestly, I'm surprised you finished the work so quickly. As payment, take this." The man handed his employee a pouch filled with gold and silver pieces. He then held up a finger. "Don't even think about turning it down. You've earned it. I also want you to take the rest of the week off to focus on preparing for the fight. Good luck."

A couple of hours later, Caladur found himself entering the arena district with Lara. Like most evenings, the district was crowded with all different sorts of people. Since he separated his life from the ROTE, he began seeing people in different ways. There were no longer three different types of people in the arena district, rather there were hundreds. Everyone had their own story and couldn't possibly fit into the simple categories that a single person forces them into.

Lara led the way since Caladur only knew his way through the exclusive parts of the arena, not the public areas. She led him through the large gates where they paid their silver piece to gain admittance. Once inside, they walked through a large hall that appeared to encircle the entire arena. At various points in this hall were exits that led to the seating sections of the arena. Lara seemed to know the exact destination she was leading Caladur to. On their way, they passed by numerous large statues of men wearing full suits of armor, save the helmet, so the people could see the faces, sculpted to near perfection. Most held long swords, a few held war hammers, and even fewer held vicious looking axes.

After slowly walking along the curve of the hallway, Lara exited the hall into the main arena. Upon entering the open area, a thunderous roar deafened Caladur's ears. He thought the hall was crowded, but that was nothing compared to the mass of people within the stands awaiting the battles to begin.

Realizing that Caladur was beside himself in the midst of the chaotic glory of the arena, Lara grabbed his hand and led him up the steep stairs. She stopped after they rose above the crowd and into the less populated section of the seating. Since it was higher, it was more difficult to see the details of the action, but the experience was much more pleasant due to the fact that you weren't surrounded by a mass of men, most of whom were drunk, spitting involuntarily as they cheered on their favorite champions.

"So what do you think?" her face was lit with joy. The electricity of the crowds triggered something inside the girl's heart.

"It's quite the experience. I don't know how I'll be able to concentrate on the battle at hand with this commotion surrounding me." He admitted.

"I've often wondered that about the champions."

"Well I can let you know soon."

"Soon?"

"Yeah. In five days, I'll be fighting down there." He decided it was time to start telling people other than Mr. Sutur that he'd actually be fighting in front of the public.

"What?" she threw her arms around the elf in excitement. "What are you fighting?"

"I don't know anything other than I'll be fighting an animal of some sort."

"What weapon will you get? How many will you be fighting?" The girl rambled off question after question about the specifics before stopping herself realizing that he already said he didn't know much of anything. "Well you've got to let me know as soon as you hear more."

"I will," he promised.

They sat waiting for the champion to enter the arena for a few moments. Then, the already enormous roar of the crowd erupted into a noise that seemed too loud to be believable. The champion made his entrance to the arena. Although he was too far away to be sure, he thought he recognized the champion as the blue champion from the foot race.

As soon as Lara saw him, her voice erupted into an ear splitting pitch that pierced the air surrounding her. She grabbed Caladur's arm and squeezed it. "He's my favorite. You'll love it. He doesn't even wear sturdy armor, yet he's never lost to any animal. He's unbelievably fast. Just watch. You won't believe what he can do."

"I've met him," Caladur stated in a simple tone as an attempt to impress her.

It worked.

"What?" She called excitedly to him over the roar. "Can you introduce us?"

"I met him once during the race around the city. I don't think I'm able to introduce you to him. After I win the apprenticeship and you paint that picture of me, I'll see what I can do."

The champion took his place in the center of the arena. Last time Caladur was inside, a mud pit sat right where the champion stood. The anticipation of the impending battle was beginning to get to Caladur.

Lara's eyes were glued to the ground of the arena, knowing that the challenger couldn't be too far away. "This will be mostly entertainment. The real, life-threatening battles aren't shown until the end of the night. He'll probably be fighting some..."

Caladur couldn't make out the rest of her explanation due to another eruption in the crowds cheers. Two large vipers entered the arena. Although Lara and the rest of the crowd knew that the antidote would be readily available for the champion if he happened to be bitten, the concoction of natural plants was nowhere near reliable enough to bet your life on.

The vipers identified their adversary in an instant. Before the snakes were released, they were poked and prodded to enrage them in order to put on a good show for the paying public. The two snakes slithered at an astounding speed towards the blue champion who was ready for both snakes. He stood on the balls of his nimble feet, ready to evade the incoming attack.

One viper raised its head to the level of the champion's mid-thigh, preparing to make an impossibly fast attack while the second viper wasted no time and slithered right at the man in an attempt to bite the champion's ankle. The blue champion rotated in order to evade the first strike while concentrating on the next. As soon as the viper made a forward motion to strike, the champion performed an acrobatic cartwheel and grabbed the snake's head with his left hand. After distancing himself from the other snake, he severed the snakes head with the false, metal thumbnail he used as a weapon. He dropped the body which slithered on the ground for a few moments before it ceased movement forever.

The champion took in the crowd's approval while he kept his wits about himself and relocated the other viper. With the beast's location known, he calculated the distance for a moment before he began sprinting towards the snake. When he was fifteen feet away, he flipped onto his hands, and then vaulted into the air where he performed a full front flip. He landed squarely on the viper's body, crushing its head and midsection with his weight. After sticking his landing, the champion threw his victorious hands into the air as he received the roar of approval.

Lara celebrated the victory with another hug. The rest of the night was in similar fashion. The champion was introduced, then the beast. Caladur watched seven different champions perform before he took his leave from the arena. It was getting late, and he assumed that Lara's father would appreciate it if he brought her back at a decent hour.

With Lara safe at home, Caladur walked through the dark night towards the slums. He entered the shack, and to his surprise, Estine and her children were nowhere to be found. After a brief moment of panic, he remembered that they would occasionally stay at Lara's home for a night. The worry persisted as he thought that Lara would have told him, but he went into his trance as he pondered ways to prepare for the upcoming event. Four more days to prepare until he would be in the midst of thousands of onlookers.

-27-

The next morning came with no sign of Estine or her children. Caladur left the small shack in the slums and made his way towards Lara's home. Before he could start training, he needed to ensure that Estine and her family, his family, were safe. He knocked on the door in a rapid manner. He was impatient and just wanted the family's safety to be confirmed. The hour was still early and many people had not yet left their homes. He knocked again.

Uncle G. finally came to the door. He didn't appear to be happy to see the elf calling upon his daughter at such an early hour. "Back already? You just saw her last night. I think you can wait until at least later this afternoon to see her again. I don't want you two getting too serious just yet. You just met her."

Caladur wanted to interrupt the man and explain that he wasn't there to see Lara, but he decided against it.

He figured that interrupting the father would only serve to further agitate the situation. When he was done, Caladur spoke. "Actually, sir, I came to make sure Estine and her children were here."

"What?" He seemed to be confused.

"Did Estine stay over here last night? They never came to the shack, and I know they stay here sometimes. I just wanted to make sure they were alright."

But Caladur knew they were not alright. He could tell by the blank expression on Uncle G.'s face that they hadn't spent the night with him.

"They weren't here. I'm sure they're alright though. Keep your eyes open and don't worry too much. They are strong and know how to handle themselves on the streets. Keep at your training. If you don't see them tonight, let me know and we can look a bit more purposefully."

"If you think that's best," Caladur conceded. "I'll be back tomorrow if I don't get any word from them." The elf took his leave and began walking the city streets in an attempt to locate Estine and her children.

Throughout the morning, he saw a few women that resembled his friend, but realized that his eyes were mistaken before calling out to them. He found himself in the storage district. It was a small section of the business district that was comprised of large, mostly empty buildings. People, farmers for the most part, would rent out the space of these buildings in the winter months to protect their equipment from the damaging snow and ice.

On his way out of this section of town, he spotted two men he recognized walking towards him a ways down the road. The elf moved towards the walls of the buildings and bit by bit made his way into a small ally that separated the buildings. Once he was deep enough into the ally to avoid any expecting eyes, he waited for the two men to pass.

It took a bit longer for them to pass than he anticipated, but eventually they did. Two males, one human, the other an elf. They both had blond hair. The elf's was straight and well kept. The human's, on the other hand, was scraggly and dirty. The two men kept pace with one another and were conversing. Caladur thought to himself, "What are Oranton and Yost doing together?"

Once the two men had passed him, he followed them from a distance. It was apparent to the elf that they were engaged in deep conversation as they continued on through the storage district, a place of the city few went on a casual stroll through. It was not public, it was not scenic, and it was not social. Caladur continued to follow. He longed to get closer to hear what the men were discussing, but he knew if got much closer, they could spot him with ease, and then they would stop their discussion for sure and deal with him. Knowing Yost's past, he didn't want to be caught in that type of situation, so he continued following from a great distance.

A while later, after he followed the men this way and that through the small district, they stopped outside of a large storage unit. Yost looked around in every direction before he opened the unit, let Oranton enter, and then entered himself before closing the door. Caladur picked up his pace and jogged towards the unit so he could try to listen in. He knew what the meeting was about. Yost was attempting to get information about the semi-finals, or he was trying to figure out how to sabotage Caladur's performance in the event. Despite his curiosity to hear what Oranton would say, he knew that Oranton couldn't help the human in any way. Oranton had no knowledge of anything within the arena. He knew a few weaknesses of Caladur, but he was confident that Yost wouldn't be able to capitalize on them.

The elf stood outside of the storage unit and was about to begin searching for a way to enter the building undetected when he heard something. A voice that was far too familiar to the elf sounded behind him.

"Caladur. We need to talk." The voice was full of regret and pain.

The young elf didn't need to turn around to see who spoke the words that once again changed his life. He didn't want to turn around. After everything that had happened in the past weeks, he didn't want to speak with her. But his heart pulled against every fiber of his being and won. He quickly turned around with his arms wide open to accept the woman into his arms.

Caladur and his mother shared a hug right there in the streets of Fatiil.

-28-

"I've missed you son," the elven woman began crying as she held her young son firm within her arms. "I can't keep this up. I don't care if I have to live in poverty, I just want to be with you. I'm so sorry Cal. You must understand that I made a mistake. One that I'll never ever make again. You need to believe me. You do believe me. Right?"

The surprise of the entire event about knocked Caladur right off of his feet. "I don't know." He had finally regained control of his body. His heart had been pushed back into his chest and his brain taken over. He muscled his way out of her arms and took a step back to stare her down. She looked no different now. Anyone walking down the streets would see her as an elegant elf. She was dressed in her fine clothes, her skin was clean, her hair was flawless. Everything about her seemed perfect. Just like any real member of the Royal Order of True Elves. But she wasn't. She was black listed just like he was. She was the one who procreated with a mixed blood.

She continued crying. "Please," she sobbed out, "at least give me a chance to explain. I can make your life right again." The tears made her sight blur, but she still saw her son in a way she never thought she'd find him. His skin battered, bruised, and covered with dust and dirt. His hair was no longer straight and elegant. Instead, it was tangled and dirty. So much so that the blonde hair seemed to be littered with brown hairs, like that of a mixed blood. Although he was wearing the same set of clothes he had been when she left him at their old home, they were battered. Holes and tears populated the stained set of clothes.

Caladur didn't want to talk to his mother. But, after seeing the pain in her face, he couldn't deny her this wish she had. "Fine. Let's go." He physically turned her around and they walked away from the storage units and into the market district. "So, what do you have to explain?"

"Everything." She had stopped crying, but her eyes were still wet and her nose was running.

The young elf gave his mother a glance, urging her to begin the story.

She took a deep breath and began telling him of her motives for abandoning him. "It all started when you beat Oranton at the True Elf Rings. Not only did you sweep the first three matches, but you physically beat him. You desecrated his face with cuts and bruises. He told me that his family teased him mercilessly the next day and he must have had something snap in his head. As his face began to heal, his heart did not. He wanted nothing more than to achieve revenge against you. And by the looks of you, he did. And I'm so sorry about that.

"He heard about our financial situation about a week before you beat him at the Rings. I had been speaking with his father and Aerandan about my monetary status, and apparently his father told him about it. I didn't know that the gift would come through. At any rate, the gift was so modest that it would have only sustained us for a month at the most. That is, if we were to keep living in the same way that we had been. I couldn't even think about telling you that you would need to wear clothes that were not perfectly, and personally, crafted for you. Anyway, Oranton's father found a family that would be interested in purchasing the home and put those wheels into motion. Once Oranton knew that we were on our way out of the home, he approached me and proposed a deal. He offered me a large sum of money if I did a few things for him. In order to receive the money, I would need to accept the small bit of money in front of the Order, I would need to slander your father and confess that he wasn't an elf, I would need to leave Fatiil with the money, and I would need to leave you here.

"At first I couldn't bear to think of leaving you here all alone. You'd be helpless in the big city. But then I thought about it. I am your mother. I couldn't think of what life would be like without you loving me. I thought that if we needed to lower our standards and live in a 'normal' home, your love for me would diminish. You would lose your friends because of me. Even though Oranton was already after you, I couldn't imagine that Aervaiel would stay with you. These thoughts scared me. I didn't want to live with you while you despised me. So, after much thought, I took the money and agreed to Oranton's terms, with the intention of securing the money, then coming back to see you."

Caladur walked down the streets without a sound, listening to his mother. The grandeur of the story she told was amazing. He wracked his brain to decide whether or not he could believe a single word she said. The woman abandoned him. There's nothing more to it. She left him all alone in the city to fend for himself. The thoughts continued firing through his mind like an army of archers taking out the front lines of the enemy. Even if she was telling the truth, how could he trust her now? How could he put his trust back in her when she could simply take another bribe to up and leave again? "So what now?" he tested the waters.

"I've come back. I want to start over. I want to find a home to buy. I want to discredit the claims I made about your father. I want to live with you again. I want everything to be the way it was."

"That's impossible." Caladur said in a plain tone.

"It may be, but I want to at least try. If it fails, I want to leave you with the money Oranton gave me. It'll be plenty for you to get back on your feet. I'll go away and never come back. If that's your decision. But I do not wish it to come to that."

"Well then you might as well leave the money and go." Caladur had heard enough. "The Order is a thing of my past. They won't allow you to return. I've already tried. It's hopeless."

"It's not Cal. I've already spoken to Aerandan. He agreed to readmit us to the Order as long as you return with me and issue a formal apology to the entire Order for your association with the other races during this time of trials."

Caladur didn't know how much he missed the Order until it was obtainable again. "Really?" The status, the cleanliness, the money. The immaterial perks that went along with being an elf were within reach once more. Then his life on the streets boiled up in his head. The arena, Estine and her family, *Sutur's This's and That's*. Lara. These thoughts were overcome as soon as he realized that these relationships were destined to end. After Tald betrayed his trust, he convinced himself that it was only a matter of time before they hurt Caladur in some way. The exhilaration of his re-admittance became unquenchable. "Alright. Let's go see Aerandan and rejoin the Royal Order of True Elves."

-29-

"So, it was Oranton? He orchestrated this entire catastrophe? I'll need to look into this to confirm that what you're telling me is true. But it shouldn't be hard to prove. It's obvious that you amassed a wealth that can easily be explained in this way." Aerandan looked over Caladur and his mother for a moment.

"Alright. You will both be readmitted to the Order on a provisional basis. There are a few stipulations that go along with this. First, I'll need an apology from both of you. First, Eruriel, you will need to confess to taking a bribe to slander another member of the Order. Even though it is your son, it is strictly against our code. In addition to this admittance, you will need to donate the bribe to the Order. Once that is complete, you will become a full member of the Royal Order of True Elves once more. Caladur, you will need to publicly apologize for associating with non-elves.

This apology must be detailed and include the names of each human, gnome, and dirty blood you spoke to during your estrangement from our Order. Obviously, you then must recommit to living a life exclusively with other elves. Finally, and this will be the most difficult. I'll need to you act civilly around Oranton. I know you were good friends. I need you to put everything that he allegedly did to you behind yourself. Until everything comes out into the open, you need to be friendly. Once his transgressions are made public, you'll be free to make your own decision regarding your association with Oranton Elennae. Are these conditions understood?"

Caladur followed his mother's lead and nodded his head in agreement.

"Good, then by this evening you will be able to gain admittance to the various establishments of the Royal Order of True Elves." Aerandan shook hands with the newest members of the Fatiilian chapter of the ROTE and dismissed Eruriel. "Caladur, I'd like to have a few more words with you. If you'd please wait."

"Sure," he replied. "I'll meet you at the True Elves Inn later tonight Mom." The elf and his mother shared a hug before she left. "Yes sir?"

"I've seen this happen over and over again throughout my life. Honestly, since I've been around, more and more of our kind have taken to associating with humans. Those who spend more than a day or so with them rarely come back. Even after they apologize and make a covenant with the Order to never associate with their kind again, they do. Sometimes in as little as a day, most after a month, some after a year or longer. After an elf associates with their kind, they are infected with a disease that eats away at them. Eventually, they will fall to the

179

sickness and once again leave the Order. It saddens me to say that you too will eventually leave us. I can see it in your eyes."

"I won't sir. I'm back to stay. I've missed the comfort and the prestige."

"I'm sure you have. It's much better than the slums I can imagine. Yet, I'm afraid you will surely fall unless you can say with every single part of your heart, your mind, and your spirit that you are here to stay and that nothing can take you away."

"I'm here." Caladur meant it. The young elf couldn't think of a single reason to leave the Order.

Aerandan stared into the young elf's eyes. "I see that you mean it. But if a shadow of a doubt ever arises within you, you must come to me immediately so we can deal with it in an appropriate way. I do not wish to lose you again. Now go on and find your friends. I'm sure they have been worried."

Estine's face flashed in Caladur's mind's eye. Caladur took no notice of the phantom thought when he made his way out of Aerandan's home. He found himself back on the streets of Fatiil. Again, he was a new man. The unfortunate humans and half bloods putted along through the streets carrying out their meaningless business. He pressed his way through the streets with his head held high. Even with this unbecoming exterior, on the inside, he was once again a full blood elf, and nothing could change it.

He was forced to turn rapidly as a human ran into his shoulder. He went along with the turn. His mind accessed the dusty corners of his mind to retrieve some insult to call to the unfortunate woman that bumped into his elven arm in an instant. His eyes caught a glimpse of the dirty, dark brown hair that flowed from the woman's head. Upon seeing the hair, his mind changed directions from searching for an insult to his memory of Lara's hair. Then her body. Then her smile. He looked down at the human and shook his head in disdain as he shoved the memory of Lara away. Without any sort of insult, the elf continued on his way down the streets of Fatiil.

-30-

Three days until the semi-finals would begin. Of course, those thoughts had left Caladur. He was an elf again, and he had no concerns for those things. To him, the Fatiilian Arena was once again a spawning pool of the miscreants of society. His night at the True Elves Inn was delightful. He was able to take a proper bath with warm water, a luxury he hadn't enjoyed for almost a month. His brand new clothes which were custom tailored for him felt perfect. Even if thoughts of the arena crossed his mind, he was able to push them aside, after a great effort, by thinking of the fine cloth sitting upon his elven skin.

He spent the night reading by candlelight, another pastime he didn't realize he had missed a great deal until he was able to experience it once more. Much of the morning was consumed by the elf cleaning himself up and preparing for the coming night. The night he would meet

Oranton and Aervaiel again. Unlike the last few times he saw them, this time, he would be an elf again, and accepted by them once more.

Noon rolled around and the properly dressed elf left his temporary home and began making his way towards Oranton's home. He knocked on the door and was welcomed with open arms by his mother. "I hear that all of the confusion has been cleared up. It's nice to see you again. I'll have Oranton down in a moment."

"Thanks." Caladur waited with patience. A flood of relief flowed over him as he was once again accepted.

Then, after a few brief moments, Oranton appeared in the doorway. "Caladur!" He exclaimed as he threw his arms around his friend. The embrace lasted for a moment. " Aervaiel is waiting for us in the Royal Pub along with a few other elves. They are excited to welcome you back. Let's get going."

The two elves walked down the streets of Fatiil, just as they always had. As quickly as his time on the streets came upon him, they disappeared, as if they had never happened. The memories were simply out of a bad dream. The pair of elves walked through the slums. On their way, they came across many men begging for money so they could afford yet another bit of food.

Caladur did his best to avoid eye contact with the beggars as he tried to protect himself from the soft center of his heart. Oranton, on the other hand, was just as spiteful as ever. He approached one of the men and dropped a handful of rocks into the man's wooden cup after making him believe it was handful of coins. He began laughing and shared the joke with his friend. Caladur struggled to come up with a laugh at first, but after he started, he forgot about his soft spot. The rest of their journey through the slums was simple for Caladur. He was able to look at each and every beggar in the face and despise them for making the streets of his city unclean.

Oranton led Caladur the long way towards the Royal Pub. He didn't go through the arena district, to Caladur's delight. The renewed elf wouldn't have to face the familiar faces in that section of town. He wasn't quite ready for that. Their trek through the city was uneventful after Oranton had properly reacquainted Caladur with the real slums of Fatiil. They found themselves approaching the Royal Pub. The last time Caladur had tried to enter the pub, he was beaten and spit upon, this time, he was granted access. The place was just as wonderful as he remembered. Despite the early hour, the pub was filled with other elves, ready to welcome the young elf back into their society.

He spent most of his time talking with Oranton and Aervaiel, who were still romantically involved. He kept many of his experiences to himself, but he did share stories of his participation within the Fatiilian Arena. As he retold the stories, he placed an emphasis of the struggles he went through and the horribleness of the human race, especially Yost. He also told of Tald's betrayal. All of the elves cheered when the idea that human's are not loyal came up within Caladur's tale.

The elves were sympathetic for Caladur and shared their condolences. As the afternoon began turning into early evening, many of the elves began to make their way towards the meeting hall of the Royal Order of True Elves. The meeting was set to begin in an hour and Caladur was expected to make his formal apology to the Order at the meeting.

Caladur left the Royal Pub with Oranton and Aervaiel. Although he expected to be jealous of the couple when he saw them together, he didn't really care. It was apparent to him that they were happy together. They shared something he never had with her while they were together. He thought about what they had as they walked through the city and at last realized what it was. They shared an absolute hatred for anyone who didn't have exclusively elven blood. As a member of the Order, it was expected that you have a general distaste for non-elves, but not necessarily hatred. Yet, as they walked merrily through the town, they wouldn't go more than a few moments before insulting a person with a small hint of elven blood.

The newly reinstated elf laughed along with them. Although he didn't agree with everything his friends were saying, he wasn't going to risk being back on the streets for the feelings of a mixed blood.

The threesome continued on their way through the city before Oranton stopped the group. "This is the place I told you about Aervaiel. The shop where Caladur used to work while he was one of them. Tell her," he prodded at his friend. "She didn't believe that I broke the window."

Caladur took a few calming breaths as he looked upon *Sutur's This's and That's*. His experiences working in the store came back to him.

"C'mon. Tell her that I did it."

The elf remained speechless. He thought about the man who financed his life while he was on the streets. The man who was nice enough to give him a break from work every day to sip on a warm cup of tea.

"Caladur. Tell her." Oranton's voice changed. His joking manner had been replaced with a belligerent tone. "Tell her that I broke the window. Tell her that it's only because of me that there's this piece of wood here covering the shattered glass."

Caladur focused all of his being on self restraint. He was about to admit that Oranton broke the window, but then Oranton began talking again.

"Tell her that the man had to hire some so-called artist to paint it. I mean c'mon couldn't he spare a few gold pieces to hire a real artist? I mean, look at the way the stones are shaped. And this, what even is,"

Oranton was cut off when Caladur's fist made contact with his mouth. Two teeth flew out of Oranton's mouth to the dirty ground. Living on the streets made Caladur stronger. Aervaiel screamed and backed away. Caladur took no notice. He jumped on the disbelieving elf and began pummeling him. Punch after punch, the elf's face became less and less recognizable.

Oranton was screaming at his friend to stop. The townspeople were watching. No one wanted to risk their personal health to save an elf who had taunted many, if not all of them. Caladur continued working on the limp elf until he was finally pulled off of his friend's unconscious body.

"Caladur. Caladur! Stop it! Get off of him!" Mr. Sutur held the frantic elf firm within his arms. The man somehow managed to hold onto the adrenaline filled elf and calm him down. Once Caladur had some reason again, Mr. Sutur ordered him into the shop. He then helped Aervaiel carry Oranton's body into the shop. Lastly, he closed and locked the doors.

The crowd outside dispersed and the Fatiilian guard was turned away by Mr. Sutur when they responded to commotion. The man prepared some tea for the elves as he began doing his best to nurse Oranton back to consciousness.

It may have been the skilled touch of Mr. Sutur, or the scent of the warm tea, but after a few minutes, Oranton came back to consciousness. The elf stood up and, without a word of thanks to Mr. Sutur, ordered Aervaiel and Caladur to accompany him to the Order's hall for the meeting.

Both elves followed the young, bloodied elf through the streets of Fatiil to the meeting hall.

-31-

The three elves entered the meeting hall of the Royal Order of True Elves just before the service was about to begin. Oranton and his beaten face led the two others through the mass of elves. He ignored the words of concern and pressed on, taking no notice. In the hall, he continued his hurried pace in a beeline to the front of the hall where Aerandan Talvir was preparing to begin the service. A drip of blood fell from Oranton's face to the floor.

"Oranton!" He was concerned. "What happened?"

"We need to talk," the elf looked around the hall to see everyone staring at him. "In private."

"Alright. You and Caladur come with me. Aervaiel, go ahead and take a seat. This shouldn't be more than a moment or two."

Everyone followed their orders. Caladur and Oranton were led by Aerandan into another room of the Order's hall.

Neither of the two young elves had ever been inside. It was not as majestic as the rest of the hall, but it was finely decorated, Aerandan wouldn't have had it any other way. The head elf took a seat in his comfortable chair behind a wooden desk that was crafted with the touch that only a trained and practiced gnome could manage. Caladur found it ironic that the desk wasn't elven made, but he didn't let his amusement show. Aerandan motioned for the two other elves to take a seat on the other side.

"Now then, what is this about?" He finally said after releasing a rather large sigh.

"Look at me. Doesn't that tell you enough?" Oranton pleaded with his leader. "He's done it again. Disfigured me. This time, he took two teeth from me." The young elf opened his bloodied mouth and pointed out two empty spaces that should have been occupied by teeth.

"Is this true Caladur? Did you do this?"

He didn't have time to think. He didn't need to. Ever since he was pulled off of Oranton by Mr. Sutur, he knew that he no longer belonged with the elves. "Yes. He was insulting the people who took care of me while you all turned your backs. He was trying to get me to speak poorly of them. And I couldn't. I wouldn't." He stopped his official statement and turned towards Oranton to address him directly. "They are better people than you could ever hope to be. That man saved your life and you couldn't even thank him."

"That's enough Caladur." Aerandan stood up to begin his decree. "Caladur Vandel, you are now, and forever, excommunicated from the Royal Order of True Elves. I would ask that you leave the premises immediately and share no words with the other elves. Do not address your mother in any way. She doesn't need to have a change of heart before she makes the right decision. Just leave."

Caladur sat there, smiling. He knew he had made the right choice.

"Now!" Aerandan roared. The middle aged elf was able to produce a frightening sound when he was agitated enough to do so.

Caladur began to slowly stand up and make his way towards the exit. On his way out, he listened as Aerandan spoke to Oranton.

"You listen to me and you listen good. You got lucky here. If that boy had enough pride to stay with us, you'd have a lot to answer for. If his mother makes your actions public, I'll have no choice but to discipline you. You'd better hope that,"

The elf continued lecturing Oranton, but Caladur had left the room. He didn't care that Oranton would be let off with a stern warning. All he cared about was that he was happy. His smile stretched from ear to ear as he walked out of the Royal Order of True Elves' meeting hall. That part of his life was, at last, behind him. Now, he could move on to the things that made him happy. He could continue working with Mr. Sutur, he could see Lara and Estine, and most importantly, he could finish his competition at the arena for the position of Rundor's Apprentice.

-32-

With the Royal Order of True Elves behind him, Caladur had two full days to train before the day of his battle within the arena. His ties with Tald had been destroyed and he had no one to train with. He spent most of the time focusing on strength training. With the money he was given by Mr. Sutur, he was able to buy admission to one of the few training complexes within Fatiil.

Although he could work out on his own, the equipment at these facilities would help him train in the most effective ways. The facility he found to work out at had some of the best utilities in the city. It came complete with short sections of iron that weighed different amounts so that as someone trained, they could increase or decrease the weight. Bars were also installed so that pull-ups could be performed. Various degrees of inclines could be used to help with the resistance applied during sit-ups. Finally, a circular track encircled the workout area.

Caladur utilized this facility both days in hopes to enhance his performance in the arena. He favored the steel bars over the other equipment. The elf felt that the versatility that came along with the free weights was most beneficial for his purpose. In addition to his work at the training facilities, he made sure to practice being sociable with the people at the gym as well as those who he met on the streets of Fatiil. He knew that a large portion of advancing to the finals would be his crowd appeal. For that reason, he made sure he spent a lot of time conversing with strangers, and making friends.

Despite his attempts, he made few friends. He had the most luck as he hung out with Lara and her friends. Yet, when they were together, it was first and foremost to search for Estine and her children. Caladur hadn't seen the family since the beginning of the week. He had no knowledge of them going on a trip, and Lara's family had not heard of one either. Although Uncle G. showed little concern, he allowed Lara to spend more time than normal with Caladur as they walked the city's streets looking for any information about Estine and her children. To their displeasure, they were unable to gather any information about the location of Estine and her children.

The young couple didn't spend their whole time searching for Estine. They had their share of fun as well. They spent one night at the arena. Lara cheered on the champions while Caladur made mental notes of various actions the champions performed in order to make the audience erupt into hoots and cheers. That night, Caladur met many of Lara's friends, the ones she had spent her childhood with. Most were humans. A few of the girls had a trace of elven blood, but nothing more. He had fun meeting the friends, he managed to get along with most of them, and, according to Lara, he received their stamp of approval. Although it was unheard of within the Order, Caladur was informed by Lara that before a girl could start a relationship with a guy, he needed to receive the approval of the girl's good friends.

When he was told this, his face turned the shade of the sun as it set over the horizon. Lara just giggled like the cute girl she was.

Caladur settled into the shack which he now considered to be cozy as he waited with unmatchable anticipation for the next day. To his chagrin, Estine, Lucas, and Celeste remained missing, but he couldn't let his mind dwell on that. After he moved onto the finals, he would be able to focus on their whereabouts in a more complete manner. Now, he needed to win. He couldn't bear to see someone like Yost, or even Tald, become Rundor's Apprentice. He needed to focus. He needed to win.

-33-

Caladur Vandel broke out of his trance with a grin the next day. He managed to push the thoughts of everything but the challenge at hand away from his mind. Mr. Sutur, Estine, Lucas, Celeste, and Lara were not important to the young elf. What mattered to him was winning the honor of being Rundor's apprentice. The elf left the shack in his still somewhat clean, fine clothing and made a direct line towards the training facility he had been working out at. Caladur spent an hour performing a light workout to prepare his body for the coming battle. With that out of the way, he walked towards the arena.

The young competitor entered the champions' entrance and descended into the bowels of the arena. Caladur was the first champion to come to the training room. He took a seat and waited. Seconds turned to minutes, which turned to over an hour. Finally, Yost entered the room, followed by Tald and Mitlo a moment later. The four challengers were present and ready for the battle to begin.

Rundor, in his typical fashion entered the room through his door a moment or two after the men were settled. "Today is your day. Whether or not you move on, you'll still have had the rare honor or fighting within the Fatiilian Arena. People throughout the country will marvel at your tales for the rest of your lives. The order of the fights has already been determined. Mitlo will fight first, then Yost, then Caladur, then Tald. Before you enter the arena, you will reach into this pouch and pull out a token. The token will represent the beast you will be fighting.

"As I mentioned before, this will be a fight to the death. The beast will not stop its assault unless it is killed or severely wounded. You'll have our help should something get out of hand, but remember, your life is on the line here. Fight well and perform well. Your battles will be the first of the night. Remember, the crowd wants a show. Let's give it to them.

"Now, before you enter, you must be equipped with armor and a weapon. If you'll follow my page, he'll show you where you need to go. I'll see you in a while, after you are prepared for your battles."

Just as Rundor was leaving the room, his page entered and beckoned the men to follow him. The young boy led the men through the lower levels of the arena with confidence. The maze of passages seemed impossible to navigate, but Caladur knew if he became a champion, he would have plenty of time to learn his way around.

The men were silent as they followed. After their falling out at dinner the previous week, Tald had nothing to say to Caladur. Mitlo had been a loner for most of the competition, and Yost wasn't about to brag about his most recent tactic in front of the other men. The dim passages seemed to continue on and on as they pressed through them.

Finally, after a long walk, the men came upon a large, dimly lit room. It was equipped with everything that the training facility had. Although the room was empty of people, Caladur could tell that the equipment was utilized habitually by the champions of the arena. In addition to the strength training tools, the room was stocked with multiple racks of different sorts of armor in all different sizes. Next to the armor shelves sat racks full of weapons in various sizes and shapes. Then, on the far end of the room stood straw targets to practice archery and crude, wooden statues that appeared to have been repeatedly struck by the weapons sitting on the rack.

"First, find a suit of armor that serves you. There's everything from leather to plate, just figure out what type fits your style the best. Once you're done, choose your weapon. Everything here is up for grabs. We ask that you stick to one weapon seeing as it takes a great amount of skill to wield two edged weapons simultaneously. If I were you, I'd avoid any bows, they are effective, but the crowd doesn't seem to appreciate those battles as much. Take your time. When you are done, feel free to warm up and make final preparations for your battle. Rundor will be down shortly to assign each of you a beast." The page boy left the hopeful apprentices alone while they began preparing for their semi-final battle.

By the time Rundor came, each man had donned their chosen armor and taken their weapon. Mitlo wore the heaviest armor that was available and wielded a long sword. Based on Caladur's observations of the fights, this was the typical arrangement of a champion. Yost had donned a suit of armor that was, for the most part, leather, but had a few installations of metal. Besides the armor, he also selected a pike, a long staff with a dreadful spear tip and a small crescent shaped ax on the top, for his weapon. Tald, like Mitlo selected a suit of sturdy, metal armor that he fit inside. Unfortunately, due to his size, he didn't have much of a choice. It was either the full plate or nothing. The short human selected a short sword to accompany his armor. Finally, Caladur selected a suit of chainmail armor. It was heavy enough to block attacks from the beast he would fight, but he was still able to maneuver quite well within it. The elf selected a short sword as his weapon. It was sharp enough to cut through whatever he was facing, but light enough to wield effectively with one hand. He considered selecting a metal quarterstaff, but realized that without an edge or point of some sort, it would not fair too well against a beast. His previous experience in the True Elf Rings would not serve him in this encounter.

In the order they were going to fight in, they each reached into Rundor's sack to retrieve the token representing the animal they would fight. The leather sack was quite large, it could hold about a gallon of liquid if it was filled to its maximum volume. A thin piece of leather was threaded through the top of the sack providing the keeper with a way to secure the contents within. Mitlo was first. He reached his hairy arm into the sack to retrieve a small copper coin with an engraved depiction of a bear. He seemed to be pleased with his selection and returned to the ranks of the other men. Yost was next. He approached the sack with confidence, dug around for a moment and then pulled out a coin with a boar impressed. Caladur pulled out a coin of the bull. Lastly, Tald secured the coin of the tiger.

The champions fought one battle at a time. When their companion was fighting, they were not allowed to observe, they were required to stay in depths of the arena, making final preparations for their own fight. Mitlo had no time to prepare. He was led by Rundor down a hallway towards the arena. Tald immediately made his way back towards the weapons rack to swap his short sword out for a pike. The long, speared tip weapon would be much more effective against a tiger than a short sword.

Yost walked up to Caladur to share a few words while Tald was busy surveying the arms. "Funny how I got a boar isn't it?" He laughed a bit. "My guy got me this coin from the arena yesterday. Overall, it was a small price to pay for the peace of mind. I palmed the coin in my hand when I put it in the bag and, then, I couldn't believe that I managed to pull out a boar, by far the easiest beast of the lot. Now I can focus on putting on a good show instead of fending for my life. Just thought you'd like to know." Yost patted Caladur on the back as he sauntered away.

Shortly after their conversation, Mitlo entered the room again. He appeared to be bruised up a bit, but he was smiling nonetheless. Before anyone had a chance to speak to Mitlo, Yost was escorted to the arena for his battle. Mitlo rested while Caladur and Tald sat on opposite ends of a bench, preparing their minds in silence for the event that was about to come.

Yost's battle lasted longer than Mitlo's. But when he came back, the faint roar of the crowd could be heard. Simply based on that, Caladur and Tald knew that Yost had performed better than Mitlo. The bar had been set for Caladur. If he beat Yost, he would be moving on. If he did worse than Mitlo, he would be finished. And if he managed to get between them, it would be up to Tald to decide Caladur's fate.

The elf took his place beside Rundor as he made his way through the passageways beneath the arena once more. After a short walk, he was stopped.

Rundor addressed Caladur personally for the first time. "Caladur. You've come a long way. I want you to know that I have faith in you. Know that I know it took a lot to turn away from the Royal Order of True Elves. I know how committed you are to this process. Since I am aware of this, I find that it is necessary to tell you that I see the fire in you. I've seen it since the second day of the tryouts. Even if you do not obtain my apprenticeship, you'll go on to do great things within the Fatiilian Arena."

Caladur nodded. He didn't know what else to do. One of the most popular champions of the Fatiilian Arena had just given the elf the best compliment he could ever hope to receive. But he couldn't let that get in his way. He knew that he needed to focus on the battle. Fighting a bull would be no easy task. He knew that the beast was fast and packed a powerful punch. He was beginning to wish that he had swapped out his weapon, but it was too late for that.

The roar of the arena hit him like a flow of rushing water that enveloped his body. The bright sun seemed to focus its rays on the young elf. He began to sweat. While he walked towards the center, the chain mail armor pinched his skin through his clothes. He did his best to put on a smile as he waved towards the massive audience in his attempt to put on a good show.

Caladur kept his eyes open to all sides as he waited for the angry bull to make its appearance. Finally, a gate directly in front of Caladur rose, and a bull that didn't waste any time, came charging out with only one thing in his mind, kill Caladur. The young elf stepped to the side of the first charge while he gauged the bull's speed and realized that a single, solid strike from the beast's horns could put him out of commission.

He poised his sword at the ready while the bull made its second attempt to attack the elf. Again, he dodged to the left, but this time, he cut a gash into the side of the bull.

The bull continued his charge and took little notice of the pain as he made a third pass.

Caladur heard the crowd cheering as the bull came around again. This time, Caladur wasn't messing around. He dodged to the right and stabbed the beast with all of his might.

The bull pressed on with its charge and so did the sword. Now, the bull was injured and ready to stop the pain. He bucked a few times to try to evict the sharp pain sticking within his ribs, yet he was unsuccessful. The sword was buried a good eight inches into the bull's massive torso. He turned, kicked up the dirt twice, and then made another attempt to trample the now weaponless elf.

Caladur began to panic without a weapon. The bull was charging at him head on. He focused on avoiding the charge and did so, but he still held no weapon.

The crowd was cheering.

Caladur knew they were enjoying his presentation, but he needed to finish the fight. He bent at his knees, ready for the next charge. The bull drew closer once again. Once near, Caladur put as much force to his feet as he could muster. The elf jumped up as he attempted to mount the angry bull. His left leg managed to clear the bulls head, but his right became tangled within the bull's horns. A dull pain erupted through his leg as his floppy body hung on the top of the bull.

The beast began to buck and Caladur thought his journey within the arena had come to an end. He spotted a couple of the champions protected behind gates ready their weapons to storm the beast and save the elf's life. But they didn't come yet. He still had a chance to recover.

The bull bucked his rear legs once, then twice. As he arched his back to buck a third time, Caladur managed to grab onto his sword.

Caladur hung onto the sword with all of his might. When the bull's legs were forced back to the ground by gravity, Caladur kept his feet wrapped around the bull's horns and pulled the sword through the bull's flesh. He heard the bull moan before it fell to the ground, dead.

Caladur got to his feet as quickly as could, removed the sword from the bull's corpse, and rose his bloodied weapon above his head. The roar of the arena once again exploded to approve of Caladur's performance. He couldn't be sure, but he was worried that the applause for Yost may have been louder. Regardless, it wasn't in his hands anymore. He left the arena in the way he entered and made his way back to the armory and training room below. As soon as he was out of the public's view, he began limping a bit. His right ankle was weak from the bull's attack.

He put on a half fake smile as he met the other men in an attempt to intimidate Tald before he entered the arena. The three competitors, who had already fought, waited in silence for Tald to return. Time drifted by bit by bit as they waited. And waited.

Mitlo looked defeated as he sat upon the bench. He was the first man to break the silence. "Congratulations Caladur."

The elf was taken off guard. He was still reflecting upon his battle with the bull.

"I heard a better reaction to your fight than Yost's. And I'm sure he did better than me. No matter how well Tald does, you're getting through."

"Really?" He asked, surprised.

"Yeah. Congrats again. You deserve it."

The silence returned while the men awaited the return of Tald.

After a long wait, Tald was carried into the room by two champions. A doctor was by his side, taping up cuts and gashes covering the naked body. The three participants sat in horrific silence while the doctor and champions continued working on the short human. A few moments later, a woman and two young children came running into the room.

"Daddy?" one of the young boys called as he ran to the wounded man's side.

"He's going to be alright. He needs some air right now," the doctor explained.

The woman nodded and gathered her children around her. Caladur overheard the doctor sharing a few more words with the woman. "He'll take a few days to heal up, but he'll survive. He won't look the same, the scars will cover much of his body. But he'll be fine."

The wife's eyes were streaming as she nodded in understanding.

The commotion began to die a few moments later when Rundor entered the room.

"Yost. Caladur. I'll see you both in one week. You'll be fighting each other for the position of my apprentice. That's all you get. I'll see you both then." Rundor dismissed Yost, Caladur, and Mitlo from the area while the doctor worked on the man with severe injuries.

-34-

While Caladur was leaving the arena, he was ambushed by Lara and her family. The girl jumped at the elf and wrapped her arms around his sore torso. "You did great!" she said before burying her face in his shoulder.

The elf smiled awkwardly as her father stared at their embrace with his eyes which were barely approving. "Thanks," he said in an attempt to cue Lara to relinquish her hug. It worked, but only after another brief moment.

Uncle G. smiled and took a step towards Caladur to shake his hand. "You did well. Slightly, unconventional, but you killed the bull. A thought came to him. "Hey. Is there any chance that we could get the bull? You know, we could have quite the celebratory feast."

"Dad," Lara cautioned with her pretty eyes.

"What?" he asked defensively.

She just glared.

"Anyway. Caladur. We'd like to welcome you to our home for dinner tonight. You've earned it."

"Thank you," he replied. Food was something he would certainly enjoy. His exhausted body was beginning to slow down. After his quite literal run in with the bull, and seeing Tald's severely injured body, he needed something to take his mind away. He decided that the combination of a warm dinner and Lara's company would pay the bill.

The family led Caladur to their home, a place he had now visited many times. The inside smelled delightful. The scent of pork chops, mashed potatoes and butter flowed through the warm home. The family of three and Caladur took their seats around the table.

The conversation focused around Caladur's experience in the arena. Uncle G. told the stories of the other participant's battles.

"The first fight was over too quickly. The champion made quick work of the bear. The second fight was very entertaining. Although he only fought a boar, he put on a great show."

Caladur rolled his eyes.

"Obviously you know how the third battle went. The last, was horrible. The champion seemed to be alright at first, but he was tackled by the tiger. His armor must not have been too secure. It fell off underneath the weight of the tiger, giving the beast an open season on the man's flesh. I hope he's going to be alright."

"The doctor said he'd be fine." Caladur took another bite of his meal.

Uncle G. then began asking question after question about Caladur's battle disrupting his meal.

The elf had grown tired of talking about his fight in no time and tried to change the subject to something that was, to him, a little bit more pressing. "Any word on Estine?"

With the simple question, conversation ceased. Lara's mother's eyes began to well up with tears. Uncle G. was visibly disturbed and cleared his throat in an attempt to push the approaching tears away from his eyes. Lara looked down at her plate of food and sat still.

"We went to the Fatiilian guard today. They had no news and a poor outlook. They said that there was little they could do. After I pressed them for some time, they finally at least took down a description of Estine and the children, but they said it would do little to help us find them." Uncle G. began to tear up. "I don't know what to do," he spoke with earnestness.

By this time, Lara's mother was crying alongside Uncle G. The young girl simply continued staring at her mostly empty plate.

"Listen, I've got a week off from the arena before my next fight. We can still find them. I'll be looking for them night and day. Lara, you can go ahead and draw a few pictures. I can hang them at Mr. Sutur's, and I'm sure I've got enough clout at the arena to hang a few up there. We should be able to find them."

"You don't need to," Uncle G. began.

"I insist. I wouldn't be where I am today without Estine's help. I won't stop until I find them."

"Fine. But you can't let your training for the arena go by the wayside." Despite his reluctance to accept Caladur's offer, the plan seemed to ease the pain consuming Uncle G. and his family. They knew that the elf loved Estine and the children almost as much as they did, and they knew that he meant what he was promising. The tears from Uncle G. and his wife began to slow.

"Alright," Caladur agreed in an attempt to be sensitive to the family's pain. "Now, sleep well tonight. I'll see you in the morning. It'll all be fine."

The elf retreated from the table after saying his goodbyes to the family. He didn't kiss Lara's hand that night, he felt uncomfortable showing that type of affection in front of her parents. The two did share a private smile with one another just before the elf began to take his leave from the home.

"Wait!"

Caladur turned to see Lara on her feet walking towards him. At first, he was expecting a hug or even a kiss goodbye, but he quickly dismissed that thought when he saw her parents, still upset around the table. "What's up?"

"You haven't seen my art yet," she smiled and quickly led him upstairs.

On the second floor was a hallway with four doors, two on each side. Lara quickly shut the first door on the right shut. Her fast motion drew Caladur's eyes to the door. Before the wooden door obscured his view of the room, he saw a bedroom which was cluttered with dirty clothes on the floor.

"Your room?" Caladur asked already knowing the answer.

Lara ignored the question, blushed slightly and proceeded to the second door on the left. She put her hand on the door handle and paused. "Promise not to laugh if you don't like it."

Caladur nodded in agreement.

"Promise." Her face was stone. Her eyes piercing.

"Alright. I promise," the elf said.

Lara nodded and opened the door.

The room was a complete mess. When compared to the girls' bedroom, her bedroom could be described as spotless. The walls and floor that could be seen were speckled with pain of various colors. Old posters that once decorated the streets of Fatiil were nailed to the wall, in an attempt to keep further paint from "decorating" them. The floor was covered in canvases which were covered in paint. Most of the floor pieces seemed to be failed attempts at landscapes or other works.

Once the utter chaos of the room set in for Caladur, he noticed four beautiful works nailed onto the walls. Two were flanking a window that looked out onto the streets below. Two more were hung on the wall to the right. Each work flanking the window was of a landscape. The piece on the left was the exact view from the window. Of course, the lighting and clouds were different, but aside from those insignificant variances, the art was perfect. The perspective, the way the setting sun cast low shadows on the city was captured perfectly in the depiction. The second landscape was just as good but instead of an imaginary landscape of a dense forest below a mountain range of fierce jagged peaks.

Caladur turned towards the other finished paintings in utter silence and awe. Both were portraits of humans. The first was clearly of Uncle G. Although the subject was identified with ease, there were a few flaws, mostly in the facial proportions. In particular, his eyes were ever so slightly enlarged, throwing the rest of the piece off. The other portrait was flawless. The boy's dark hair was messy but cool. A quirky smile spread across his entire face. The joy was visible in the boy's smile, eyes, and even cheeks. His brown eyes seemed to glow, even in the dim room.

"Well?" Lara finally said impatiently after allowing Caladur to peruse the work for a few minutes or so.

The elf could only mutter a single word. "Beautiful."

-35-

The week went by at a fast pace. No word of Estine or her children. Caladur spent the morning working out and preparing for his final battle against Yost for the apprenticeship while Uncle G. led the search for Estine. After lunch, Caladur would take over the search while Uncle G. went to tend to his store. Caladur then spent the rest of the afternoon, evening, and nighttime patrolling the streets of Fatiil searching for the family who reached out to him.

On the second day of the search, Lara spotted a few children of the slums playing with Celeste's rag doll. The one Caladur had given her. The children said that they didn't know where it came from and that they simply found it outside of their shack one morning a week prior. The children then told Lara that they had never met any children named Lucas or Celeste. Lara left the children in the streets playing with the doll with no more information than when she came upon them. Her hope was beginning to fade.

Lara and Caladur spent much of their afternoons and evenings together while searching. They would walk through town, holding hands as they searched. On the third evening, Caladur spotted some elves he knew from the Order walking through the city. As he looked closer, he saw that one of the elves was his mother. The thought of asking her for help crossed his mind, but he quickly dismissed it when she intentionally looked away from him. He realized that although she had given birth to him, he was now an outcast and she would never be his mother again. In a strange way, that made him happy.

Their search didn't turn anything up that night as he walked Lara back to her home.

"I really appreciate the help you've given our family through this." The girl sighed. "You've been great."

"So have you," he paused, "and the rest of your family. You've helped me realize what life is about. Without you, I would probably be one of those stuck up elves. I wouldn't care about Estine and her children. I wouldn't care about Yost cheating to achieve greatness within the arena. I wouldn't care about anything or anyone but me." He smiled, and without taking a moment to think about it, kissed her lips.

The touch was magical. The elf's body tingled as a euphoric feeling rushed through his elven blood. The kiss broke, but the feelings didn't. The couple smiled at each other and then embraced in a tight hug which ended only after another, short kiss was shared between the two.

"I should get you home."

Lara nodded.

After he dropped his girlfriend off at her home, he made his way back to the slums. He entered the shack that was his home and tried to settle down for the night. Thoughts of Lucas spinning his top ran through his mind and he was unable to enter his trance. After about thirty minutes of struggling to go into his trance, the elf stood up and began walking the streets again, trying to find Estine. Despite the horrible outlook from every public official they had spoken with, Caladur's hope, although dwindling, was still alive.

Caladur fist made his way to the business district. He thought that if Estine was still alive, she would need to be eating something. He dropped by each pub to ask the bartenders if they had seen anyone resembling Estine. The first seven bars he entered came back with a negative response. He was getting tired and about ready to give up on his search but decided to go into one last pub.

The elf entered the *Amber Ladle*, a small pub with only a few patrons within. Of the six customers, Caladur recognized one in an instant. "Owsin?" Caladur asked the man.

"Cally? Is atchu boy?"

Caladur nodded. He was a bit surprised by the fact that Owsin remembered him.

"Sit on down. Havea drink," he waved to the bartender. "Mug of ale for my frien Cally ere."

The mug was poured and delivered to the elf. "Thanks."

"So what brings aguy likeyou out 'ere this late?"

"I'm looking for a friend. They've been missing for about a week. You haven't seen a woman from the slums with two young children around have you?"

"Can't say I've seen em. Buchoo managed to finda frien. Put er there Cally."

The two men shared in a handshake before continuing their drinks.

"I guess I did. So how did you get out of prison? I came to pay your bail as soon as I had some money, but you were already gone."

"Ya did? Tanks for the thought. But like I said, my ma's got plenta money. She jes lives bout a day away so it takes a bit a time before the money can get ere. Ya know? I'm jes gettin a bit nervous. I think her times a runnin out. Ya know. She's got a bit a the sickness. I tink this mighbe er las winter comin up. Ats why I was in prison. I took too much a the ale that night. It's when I eard tha news. So I caused a ruckus. I wasn righ. But I jes got so worriedbout er. I lover so much." The man put his head on the bar and began sobbing.

The elf put his hand on the man's back and gave a little rub. "It'll be alright Owsin. You going to go visit her?"

"I don know," the man cried. "I don wanna jes leave ma job. Y'know? An my family can't jes up'n leave. There's jes too much ere. Do ya tink I can really jes leave itall an go see my ma?"

Caladur pondered the question. He thought about his relationship with his mother but came to realize that he wouldn't ever run into this dilemma throughout his life. His relationship with his mom was done, something that wouldn't ever cause a problem for him in the future. Then, he realized how he would feel if his mother came down with a deathly illness while he was still in the Order, before any of his recent trials occurred. "You should do your best to go see her."

"Tanks Cally. I knew you'd know what todo. Yer a real frien Cally. Come ere boy." Owsin wrapped his arms around Caladur and the two shared an embrace. "So what av you been upto since ma boy got choo outa the clink?"

Caladur took time to fill Owsin in on his audition for Rundor's apprentice, his life in the slums and his entire experience with the Royal Order of True Elves. The night drifted by as the two men shared stories with one another. At last, Caladur decided that he must take leave from the *Amber Ladle* and get at least some rest for the night.

"Thanks for talking with me," Caladur began standing up. "And keep your eyes open for Estine and her children. If you hear anything come find me in the slums." The elf began leaving. "Oh. And I do think you should go back home and see your mom. Come find me when you get back. If you need some help, I'll be here. I still do owe you one."

"Tanks Cally." The man grinned and laughed a bit just like he did in the prison when Caladur was a different person.

When Caladur got back to his home in the slums, he was at last able to enter his trance.

The searching continued in the same manner for the next two days. Caladur and Lara kept their relationship from her parents hoping to find Estine, and then share the news. However, nothing had been found. The only lead had been the doll and that proved to be utterly useless.

Hopes within the family were low and they were about ready to call off the search with only two days before Caladur's next fight. But then it happened. Hope was given back to Caladur and Lara in a way neither had expected.

As they were walking through the streets, back towards Lara's home. A short man with a scarred face tapped on Caladur's shoulder.

"We need to talk."

-36-

"I don't want to hear anything you have to say Tald." Caladur turned back to Lara and tried to lead her away from the man.

"Wait. Caladur."

The elf continued walking away.

"I'm sorry!"

Caladur thought to stop but pressed on. Then, Tald shouted at the top of his lungs, "I know where your friends are!" He didn't need to shout that loud, but did anyway to try to get Caladur's attention. It worked.

The young elf turned around and made a dash towards the human. As he drew near, he froze for the briefest moment as he took in the damage the tiger had done to the small man's face. Red scabs littered his head. Some had already scarred. The rest would be quick to follow suit. The man walked with the help of a cane. He was putting all of his weight on his right leg and the wooden staff. "What do you know?"

"I'll tell you, but only in private. Please, come to my home."

Caladur judged that the man appeared to be sincere. "Lara go home. I'll be there as soon as I can."

"No," she protested. "Estine's my aunt. I'm coming with you."

Caladur looked towards Tald for a response.

"Only you Caladur."

"But," Lara began again.

"Only Caladur." The short man stated bluntly, shutting down any further objection.

Lara looked at longingly at Caladur, but there was nothing he could do. They both knew that if they were going to find Estine, Lucas and Celeste, they would need to hear what Tald had to say. She left the two men to walk to Tald's home as she made her way back to her home in the northern part of the city.

"So what do you know?"

"When we get home. Before I get to that though, I need to discuss a few other things with you, for my own peace of mind."

Caladur had no other choice but to hear the man out. Although his mind didn't care, his heart hoped that he would eventually come around. He didn't spend much time with the other participants during the tryouts. He felt connected to Tald. Even after his betrayal. "What do you need?"

"First of all, I need to tell you that I'm sorry. I knew as soon as you left the diner last week that you were right. Yost was out of place to commit those acts. I guess I was just too," he paused, "too into the competition. I wanted nothing more than to become a champion, and after I heard about his actions, I immediately thought to myself 'why didn't I think of that'. It's horrible."

Caladur listened silently through Tald's extended pause as he followed the hobbling man through the city towards the middle class housing on the southern side of the city.

"I didn't consider the lives he was affecting until my fight in the arena. Well, until after it. Until after I saw the tears flowing from everyone in my family. I just about died out there. At first I thought about the family of the man he killed. Then, I thought that he must have cheated in some way. Somehow he rigged it so that he would fight a boar."

"Yeah," Caladur finally spoke. "He paid to get the coin of the boar the day before and palmed it as he reached into the bag."

"I knew it. See. Because he took the boar, it only left the more difficult beasts for us. If he wouldn't have taken the boar, I may have fought the boar instead, and he would be the one with a scarred face."

The argument didn't seem completely valid to Caladur, but he could understand where the man was coming from. And, at least he saw the errors in his judgment earlier.

"Now, I need to live with these scars to remind me of my failure."

Caladur cut the man off. "It's not a failure. It should remind you of your success. You beat out hundreds, maybe even over a thousand other men. You have fought in the Fatiilian Arena. You are a champion. You may have been scarred by a tiger, but how many of the other people in this city would have been killed. You survived a fight in the arena. Not many people can say that. Those scars mark your victory. Don't forget that."

Tald smiled. His spirit began to soar as he took a new perspective on his experience that he held onto for a long time. The short man led Caladur into a small home. "Welcome to my home, friend."

The title was accepted and Caladur entered the home. Inside, Tald's wife and children were already eating their dinner. A plate full of delicious food waited for the hero of the household to consume it.

"I'm sorry. If I'd have known we were going to have company I'd have prepared another plate." Tald's wife explained.

"No. I don't need anything." Caladur excused himself.

"Nonsense. I've got some more in the kitchen still. I'll be right back." Tald's wife left for a moment and returned with another plate with steaming food. "Take a seat and enjoy."

Caladur ate his meal with the family. He shoveled the food into his mouth. The food was delicious, but he didn't want to waste any more time. He wanted to find out about Estine. After he finished eating his food and had been properly introduced to the family, Caladur excused himself and asked to speak to Tald in the other room.

"You said you knew about Estine."

"Ah yes." The relief of getting the apology off of his chest made the man entirely forget about the woman. "Is Estine her name then? The woman that looks like she's from the slums?"

"Yes."

"And the children?"

"Lucas and Celeste. Where are they?"

"Before I get there, let me explain how I know. Go ahead and take a seat."

"Just tell me where they are." Caladur was beginning to lose his temper.

"I know you are worried. But they are safe, to an extent. Just listen please. You should know as much as possible before going in. Remember, in order to be a champion, you must be wise as well as strong."

Caladur sighed. He knew he had been beaten. The chair he sat in was made of wood and not very comfortable, but when Tald began speaking, the discomfort of the chair didn't bother him.

"It took a few days for me to heal up enough. The cane helps me walk. My left leg is pretty bad still, but I've been assured that it will heal, with time of course. Anyway, with the exception of my leg, the injuries are completely superficial and only draw attention to me in the streets. People look at me like I'm some sort of monster. The scars don't do much for business either," he added with a light hearted chuckle. "I don't think my dad wants me working for him anymore. I guess it's just what I wanted. Anyway, I knew that Yost had something to do with my pairing, whether it was direct or not. So I went looking for him.

"It didn't take long. People like him stick together. I visited a few bars where his type hang out and found him at the third. Despite my intentions, I thought better than to approach him in the middle of a bar of his friends. I was already injured. I didn't want to be killed. So I waited. I waited for him to leave the bar, which he did after an hour or so. He traveled north, past the market district and into the storage district. I kept a hearty distance between him and I until the streets cleared. No one hangs around the storage units this time of year. I was about to close the gap and approach him, when I noticed that he met with another man. A young elf, about your age."

"Oranton," Caladur said quietly.

"What was that?"

"Oranton," he said louder.

"How did you know his name?"

"I saw those two in that area last week. I didn't think much about it. I went through a lot just after I saw them. Sorry. You were saying?" He didn't want to get into another long discussion when he was this close to finding Estine.

"Yes. So, I saw them and thought it was strange. So I kept my distance. They walked around one of the units, as if they were scouting, then went in. I guess on some days, it's helpful to be short. Once they were in, I came up to the unit and found a small crack in one of the boarded up windows. I took a peek inside and spotted the woman, two children, and the elf talking with Yost. The woman and children were locked up in a cage. The elf was bringing them food and Yost stood by watching as the two men discussed their business. Basically, Yost and the elf, Oranton, were working together to get you out of the competition for Rundor's apprenticeship."

Caladur wasn't surprised. The elf held absolutely no respect for either of the men. But he wasn't going to stand by anymore. Now, it had gone too far. He stood up and began making his way to the door.

Tald did his best to get to his feet, but struggled for a moment with his cane. He hobbled after the elf, calling his name. "Wait! Caladur!"

The elf stopped. It was the least he could do. Tald was, after all, the one who found Estine. "What?"

"Don't do this. You need to get the guard. Go in with them. If you get caught up in this, the elves could put this on you in some way."

Caladur processed the thought and realized there was no way around it. He had to go to the guard and report the abduction.

-37-

Caladur and Tald arrived at the bastion a short while later. Caladur led the way. He was not only ready to free Estine and her children, but also to achieve revenge and serve justice. He had had enough of Yost and his cheating. All of that was about to end. The thought that he would become Rundor's apprentice by default didn't cross his mind. That was something he cared little about when compared to the lives of Estine, Lucas and Celeste.

The elf had only been in the bastion twice before. He had been there once as a prisoner and once to find and free Owsin, the man who stayed within the prison to let Caladur, a total stranger, out. He did not know where to go. "Where do I report a crime?" He asked the first guard he came across.

"Very end of the hall. The clerk can get you where you need to go."

By the time the guard had finished his report, Caladur was off. Tald hobbled behind as fast as he could.

"There's been a kidnapping. I know where they are being held."

That was all it took. The clerk rang a small, but loud, bell and four guards made their way to the desk immediately. "This man has the location of hostages. You four follow him."

The four members of the guard were more than ready to help. They followed Caladur and Tald out of the bastion as quickly as Tald could lead. Although Caladur had seen the storage unit, Tald had witnessed the hostages being held inside and was there earlier that evening.

The members of the guard were well equipped. Each was wearing expertly crafted full plate armor. Not the generic kind that a person could buy at any armor store, as long as they had the gold, but rather a custom fit suit of armor. It didn't appear to hinder their movement in any way. The breastplate of each suit held the crest of Fatiil painted in fine detail. Two guards carried long swords, another held a short sword. The final guard, who had mostly elven blood, carried a crossbow and had a portable battering ram around his back.

The party made their way through the market district and into the storage district. The sun had just set and the cloudy night sky lent very little light to the city. Tald identified one of the storage sheds as the place where the three hostages were being held. The members of the guard stopped for a moment to quietly formulate a plan. Tald identified the last known location of the hostages and said that there may be as many as two men within. Caladur added that both had been trained in various forms of combat.

Two of the guards lit torches. One was given to Caladur, the other was held by a guard wielding a short sword. The leader of the squad gave the signal and the elf slammed his battering ram against the wooden door. They didn't take the time to test the door, they simply burst through it.

Inside the shed, the guard made quick work of the only hostile within. The two guards wielding long swords charged forward. The young elf inside had no choice but to drop his staff and fall to the ground. One guard held him at sword point while the other secured a set of manacles around the elf's wrists.

Caladur followed the guards in, ran past Oranton and went straight to the cage where he found Estine, Lucas, and Celeste. They were safe. Each had lost a lot of weight and appeared to be in low spirits. But the appearance of Caladur seemed to change that faster than any one of them would have expected. He was pulled away from the cage by one of the guards as the archer took the battering ram once more to the door of the cage. This took a few hits, but after the third, the lock buckled and gave way to the heavy log of wood.

Estine and the children ran out of the cage and gave their hero, their champion, a hug. "Caladur!" Lucas shouted as he ran. The family held onto him as the guard took care of Oranton. Tald stood back watching.

The hug broke off and a few tears rolled down Caladur's face. "I can't believe you're alright. We had almost given up hope, but," Caladur looked behind him and waved Tald to come join him. "This man, my friend, Tald. He found you."

Estine and the children awarded the short man with a hug. Tald winced as Lucas bumped into his bad leg, but he didn't care. He just smiled and hugged the children right back. Once they released, he came to see Oranton talking to Caladur.

"It wasn't my idea," Oranton pleaded. "Yost came to me. He told me it would get you out of the tournament." The young elf was sobbing. The tears only served to further disguise his speech. His missing teeth, the ones Caladur took, gave the elf a lisp. "Yost is the bad guy. I made him promise not to kill them. They would be dead if it wasn't for me. He refused to feed them. He refused to clean the feces. I did that. I made sure they lived. They owe me their lives."

Caladur looked to one of the guards who gave the elf and approving glance.

Oranton, with his arms secured behind his back continued pleading with Caladur and the guards until Caladur's fist met his face, yet again, removing consciousness from the elf once more.

"It's about time you did that," one of the guards chuckled.

Caladur laughed in turn. "But what about Yost. The other man who helped him?"

"There's nothing we can do now. I guess we could put him before a judge, but we don't have any evidence. We only have the words of an elf who's trying to save himself, a family of the slums, and a few alleged witnesses. There's no proof. He'll be off free and it'll just waste our time. In all honesty, so will the elf. It ain't right, but that's the way the city is. Elves don't stay locked up for long."

Caladur would have been disappointed, but then he saw the smiling faces of Estine, Lucas and Celeste and knew that everything would be alright.

"Alright. We're gonna get him down to the bastion to lock him up as long as we can. You folks good?"

Caladur and Tald nodded. The guard then took their leave with the family soon to follow.

Tald said his goodbye and the children thanked him once more before he made his way home to his own family.

The elf walked with Estine and Celeste back to Lara's home while he gave Lucas a ride on his back. The young children were so weak. Celeste had just enough strength to make it to her uncle's home. However, once they drew near, the children both sprang to life. It was miraculous to witness. Their short legs carried them both to, and into the home.

Caladur and Estine heard the family scream in fits of joy a short moment after the children entered the home. They were welcomed with open arms, comfortable chairs, and as much food as they desired. Estine told of the two men that captured them, the heartless human and the elf who, at the very most, protected them from death. The two children quickly fell asleep. Celeste in the lap of Lara and Lucas in the lap of Caladur.

Uncle G. took the liberty of sharing Caladur's position in the finals of the competition at the arena that was to take place the day after next. After the joyful reunion, Estine declined the offer to spend the night. She missed her home. Even though it was little more than four walls and a partly functioning roof, it was still her home.

She led the way home with Caladur and Lara following closely behind. Both Caladur and Lara held one of the sleeping children in their arms as they walked to the slums. Estine sighed as she entered her home. "You kept it well. Thank you." She said to Caladur quietly.

He nodded in return before setting Lucas on the hard ground next to his mother. The family of three slept through the night back in their home. Outside of the shack, Caladur and Lara shared a goodnight kiss before the young woman made her way back home.

"I saw that," Estine said as Caladur went back inside.

He froze.

"Congratulations."

"Thank you," he said as relief poured over him, "and welcome home. Now get some sleep."

"You too. You've got a big day coming."

Estine drifted to sleep and Caladur entered his trance quickly.

Caladur had one more day to train before his final challenge. A fight against Yost, something he'd been looking forward to more and more as the weeks went by. Now, he could just about taste it. The trancing elf smiled in apprehension.

-38-

It was the day of the finals. Caladur snapped out of his trance right away. Lucas spoke as soon as the elf moved a muscle. "Good luck. I'll be cheering for you." The young boy spoke even though he was still half asleep.

"Thanks buddy," he said before he left the small home.

The sun was bright and warm. Not as warm as the day he first began this journey. The day of the race around the city had been just about four weeks ago. The season was slowly beginning to change into autumn. The early morning streets were bare for the most part. Every so often, Caladur passed by a merchant leaving the city early to put some miles away before the bandits that had been reportedly gathering outside of the city were up.

The young elf, now much more mature than many of the elves he used to associate with, made his way towards the market district. He first passed through the arena district where he spotted a few posters nailed to the wooden boards where announcements were placed. A few of these posters had a depiction of him and Yost fighting underneath Rundor's crest. His fight was being advertised as the main event of the arena that night. His insides jittered a bit at the thought as he continued on.

He arrived outside of *Sutur's This's and That's* a bit before his normal time. A bell sounded from above as he entered the store's main room. "Mr. Sutur! I'm back." He called.

The middle aged man came out from the back, almost running. "Well indeed you are. It's about time, as you can see the front needs a bit of cleaning."

Caladur took a look around and realized that the store was in as much disarray as the first time he had come to work in the shop.

Mr. Sutur responded before Caladur had a chance to answer. "That beautiful painting outside, where the glass window was, seems to be a hit. More and more people have been coming in ever since. See. Just like I said. Everything works out."

Caladur smiled. "So you want me to tidy up the front?"

"Yes. But not yet. First, you've got quite a bit to fill me in on. Last time I saw you, as I recall, you were about to murder an elf in front of my business. Now that is certainly not good for my store." He laughed a bit. "Take a seat, sip on some tea, and fill me in."

Caladur told his boss everything. He began with the return of his mother. He confessed to rejoining the Order and then explained the whole story of why he left. He did pass by the part of Lara painting the storefront. The elf figured that if she wanted Mr. Sutur to know, she would have told him. Caladur continued to explain his participation in the arena and about the finals tonight. Mr. Sutur already knew about the finals and had confessed to stealing one of the advertisements to keep as a momentum. Finally, Caladur shared the story of Estine's rescue and the beginning of his relationship with Lara.

In total, the conversation took about an hour and three cups of tea. After it was done, Caladur went to work in the front. He completed his work in record time. After talking about the upcoming fight, his anticipation grew. The elf worked rapidly, subconsciously hoping that time would then go by faster, it didn't work.

With his work complete, he gave Mr. Sutur a firm handshake goodbye and exited.

"I'll be there cheering for you!" Mr. Sutur called as Caladur left the store.

Caladur went to the arena and was granted access to the training room just after noon had come and gone. He worked his muscles lightly, preparing them for the battle that was getting closer and closer as time drifted by. Yost joined him in the room later that afternoon, about two hours before they were required to be there.

"I heard through the grapevine that you found your friends from the slums. Was everyone involved served their proper justice?" He winked. "You know, the elf did save their lives. If it were up to me, I would have just slit each of their throats, first the mom, then the girl, then the boy, your biggest fan, as he called himself. The little runt wouldn't shut up. Every time I went in he said, 'Caladur won't let you get away with this.' But guess what? I did. I always do. The only downside is that your mind can be focused on the fight. If I had it my way, you'd still be thinking about them as much as the fight. I'd have you distracted. But, I guess I'll just have to beat you the old fashioned way. Just like I did at the race."

Caladur's entire body wanted to fight the man and end it once and for all, right there, but his mind stopped him. He would have his time to serve the man with tangled hair and jumbled teeth proper justice, and now was not that time. It was coming. A couple more hours and he'd have his way with the man.

The two men didn't share any other words. Both practiced their archery, their swordsmanship, and kept their muscles warmed up. They both knew they would be fighting each other, but neither knew what curveballs would be thrown their way.

After hours of practice, the two men made their way to the meeting room where they were instructed to report to. Shortly after they took their seats, on opposite sides of the room, Rundor entered. He was accompanied by four other champions. Caladur had met each of the champions during the race around the city. Each was wearing their appropriate color. Blue, red, green, and purple.

"You two men have traveled a great distance, both physically and mentally, to arrive in this room today. No matter the outcome, don't take any part of your journey for granted. Whether you win and become a champion in the Fatiilian Arena, or you lose and go on to do other things with your life, remember the struggles you've overcome, and the achievements you both have obtained. It has not been an easy road for either of you. My fellow champions were kind enough to come share a few words with each of you before you compete tonight."

The blue champion was the first to speak. "The flow of the rivers has rushed through each of your bloodlines. It is a power that can be utilized both offensively, as well as defensively. Do not take this gift lightly. The dexterity each of you holds will prove to help you escape the most dangerous situations you may find yourself in. Both inside and outside of the arena." The blue champion left the room.

"The power of fire is unmatchable. Without the power, without the force, you will not succeed as a champion. Attack hard, hit harder. Without some muscle behind your attacks, you'll surely find your end."

As soon as the red champion left the green took a step forward. "The everlasting endurance of nature is unobtainable, but must still be your goal. Any champion who lacks in endurance will soon find his demise. Keep fighting, no matter what. You've both proven yourselves in this area. Remember that and you will be able to last." The green champion paused, took a deep, soothing breath, and left the room.

The purple champion was the last remaining. The elderly, human woman began speaking to the men, but somehow, Caladur knew she was speaking directly to him. "Wisdom is the most important attribute you must possess. It's one thing to know how to hit precisely, or to hit hard, or even to hit consistently over time. However, the ability to have a presence of mind while committing such acts is what truly separates the champions from the members of the guard. In order to succeed in this, you must be wise and keep your wits about yourself. If you can do that, you'll surely succeed." The woman in the purple paused for a moment and looked at each of the participants for a few moments. "It's strange seeing the two of you here at this stage. For a woman of my age, I've got quite the memory. Elf, I remember you like the race was yesterday. Human, I can't say that I've ever seen you before in my entire life."

233

The woman hummed to herself as if she was thinking, but Caladur was aware that she knew exactly what had happened on the day of the race.

"That said, I'd like to remind you both one very important aspect of wisdom. And that is the wisdom of fighting a fair and honest fight." The focus of the speech was now on Yost. "It seems like common sense to me, but if you need to cheat to obtain something, will you be able to properly utilize it once you obtain it?" She let the thought linger as she stared deep into Yost's eyes. After a moment, she took her leave from the room, leaving Rundor alone with the final two participants.

"You each must take each of their bits of wisdom to heart. Without each of those four pieces, you will be unable to perform well as a champion, even if you do win the competition today. Speaking of the competition, I bet you are both wondering what the specifics will be. First, and foremost, this will not be a fight to the death. You two might as well consider yourselves fellow champions for the night, and as you both should well know, a champion would never take the life of another champion. We are a brotherhood. A brotherhood that one of you two will join by the end of the night. If one of you kills the other, both will be disqualified from the competition.

"That being said, I'd also like to say that if I find either of your tactics in any way 'cheap' I'll declare the other man the victor. I'll declare a winner when one of two things occurs. If I feel that one of you has clearly won the battle, I will declare a winner. The other way to win is by knocking the other man out, but keep in mind, if you kill your opponent, you will be removed from the competition. Are there any questions?"

Neither man spoke up.

"Alright. Go ahead and prepare yourselves. I'll collect you from the armory when it's your turn to fight." Rundor left the two men alone in the room.

Caladur led the way as the two men walked to the armory.

"I guess I won't be killing you then." Yost declared.

The elf took no notice of the man's words. His entire mind was consumed with the battle.

Once he arrived in the armory, Caladur assembled his battle gear. He put on the same suit of chainmail he utilized during the last battle. With his armor secured, he selected a pike from the rack. The long, wooden staff of the weapon was similar to the quarterstaff he felt most familiar with. The spike and the small ax head wouldn't hurt his chances in the battle either.

Yost put on a suit of full plate armor and grabbed a long sword from the rack.

The two men waited in silent anticipation for Rundor to collect them for their battle.

When the time for battle to begin came, Rundor entered the room. The two participants then made their way to the arena to secure their position as Rundor's apprentice.

Most of the crowd was shrouded in the darkness of the night. A ring of torches encircled the arena which granted just enough light for the audience to see the stadium. Caladur looked up into the crowd. He could only see the first few rows, but despite the mass of people, he found himself able to identify a group of spectators making an enormous amount of noise. He was able to spot Mr. Sutur, Lara and her parents, Estine, Lucas and Celeste and Tald, along with the rest of his family.

He shook the excitement of the audience out of his system and focused on his opponent. The fight began a moment later when an archer shot a flaming arrow from one side of the arena to the other.

Yost charged at Caladur who had his pike poised, ready to spear the charging man. As he drew closer, the jumbled mess of teeth inside Yost's mouth appeared as the human smiled. He continued his charge, taking no notice of the spear tip that glanced off of his armor as he swung his sword at Caladur's stomach. The sword made contact with the metal armor. The force made Caladur bend over to the front.

As Yost brought the hilt of the sword down towards Caladur's head, he performed a summersault, narrowly dodging the blow. The elf got back to his feet just in time to step to the side of a powerful stab. The elf realized that his edged weapons would do little good against the heavily fortified armor that Yost was wearing. He resorted to the staff of the polearm to mount his attack. He brought the wooden shaft across the side of his adversary's helmet. A gong-like sound emitted from opened areas, and based on Yost's movement, the blow had been effective. Caladur attacked with another strike causing a similar result.

Yost distanced himself from the elf after making a powerful swing and removed his helmet. Not only was his vision impaired by the helmet, the sound it produced whenever he was struck shook his entire body. With a better view of his opponent, he made another attempt to make another effective strike. Once again he missed. The elf was too fast, he'd never be able to land a blow with the heavy armor weighing him down. Yost unbuckled his bracers and worked his way all the way up to his breast plate. With every piece that came off, his mobility was increased by a drastic increment.

Caladur's opponent was now only protected by his greaves. The rest of his body was covered only by common, thin clothes. The elf's strategy changed. He began aiming at the man's appendages with the small ax as he tried to land strikes that would cause pain, but not lethal damage. The precision aim and mastery of his strength was necessary to perform that type of particular attack. Not to mention that he needed to keep his opponents long sword in mind as well.

Yost had been cut on his left arm twice and his right once. His ability to properly wield the long sword was quickly diminishing along with his hopes of victory. The elf, despite the bruises that were surely forming underneath the chainmail, was still fighting as if he had not suffered a single blow.

The human placed the entire fight on the line, dropped the long sword and lunged, headfirst at his adversary.

Caladur had been taken to the ground, Yost was above him. The man's breath was the worst thing he had ever smelled. A fist made contact with his face. Then a knee to his ribs. That was quickly followed with another punch across his face.

"Feel familiar?" Yost taunted as he put another knee into the elf's side.

The two men were grappling in the center of the arena. Despite the hundreds of torches, very little light made its way to the center. The audience cheered as loud as they could even though they couldn't see what exactly was happening.

Another knee to Caladur's side.

"Guess I'm going to win," Yost spit in Caladur's face before bringing one final strike to Caladur's head.

The elf stopped his struggle and the arena went dark, along with his hopes and dreams.

-39-

The next day, Caladur left the shack in the morning. He was quite sore from the fight, but he would recover. It almost seemed that the fight had been a dream, but the pain he still felt throughout his body reminded the elf that he had lost. Yost was awarded the position of Rundor's apprentice. Caladur did not remember the official announcement, but he was waking up in the middle of the slums after being knocked unconscious by the pitiful excuse for a man. He knew he had lost.

The elf exited the shack and began making his way towards *Sutur's This's and That's*. But he never made it that far. While he was passing through the arena district, he was stopped by an old woman he recognized as the purple champion.

"Good morning," her voice was full of life, unlike the empty streets. "Where are you off to at this hour?"

"Work. I've been helping out at *Sutur's This's and That's* to make a bit of money while I competed.

"You are quite the young man," she marveled. "I've never seen a man, let alone one as young as you, make it this far while continuing to work on the side. It's quite remarkable."

"Thanks," but he knew he still lost, and that was all that mattered to him.

"You know, I'm not dumb. I know Yost is the man who assaulted you in the race. I bet that feels like forever ago for you." The woman snorted a cackly laugh to herself. "It's funny how the cheaters come out on top sometimes. But don't you worry. He'll fall from his high soon enough."

"Yeah," Caladur agreed to be polite.

"As a matter of fact, that time is coming a bit quicker than you may expect." She paused to let the idea sink into Caladur's mind. "Do you think Mr. Sutur would mind if you arrived an hour or so late to work? There's something I'd like to show you."

Caladur knew that Mr. Sutur would be offended if Caladur didn't go to see what the woman was going to show him, but he wasn't sure he wanted to go. After a mental debate, the word "sure" came out of his mouth.

"Follow me."

The woman led the elf into the audience section of the arena where they took a seat near the bottom. The arena was completely empty with the exception of some garbage that blew this way and that in the wind.

"What is there to see?" the elf questioned after a few moments of silence.

"They'll be here shortly." The old woman put her hand on the elf's leg. "Be patient."

Caladur breathed steadily as the cool wind blew across his face. His long, blonde hair tossed this way and that as the air pushed it. His eyes took in the massive wonder of the enormous structure he sat within. Then, two men entered the large arena. Rundor and Yost. Neither men were wearing armor, but each carried a quarterstaff.

"I'm sorry, but I'd rather not see what I'm missing out on." Caladur tried to stand, but the woman's powerful hand held his knee down.

"You won't want to miss this. Trust me."

Caladur remained in his seat.

"Like I said, I knew what he did to you on the day of the race. I told Rundor, and now he knows. Apparently, last night after the battle, Tald, one of the other participants told Rundor about Yost's involvement in the kidnapping of a family from the slums. I don't know if you know this, but Rundor, too, was originally from the slums."

"So what is all this about?"

"Patience Caladur. Just watch."

The elf couldn't hear what was being said, but he did notice that Yost had spotted him in the seating. He wasn't positive, but he thought the man winked at him from the distance. After Rundor and Yost held a brief conversation, they began sparring with the staffs. Although Yost was unaware, Rundor was moving the battle from the center of the arena towards the wall where Caladur and the purple champion sat. In every single bout, Rundor bested Yost. The man had been hit with a swift, powerful blow by the champion about seven times before they were at the wall. When they were near, Rundor attacked Yost, and easily put him into a hold, leaving Yost defenseless. Then, once Yost was secured, the champion addressed Caladur.

"I've heard that this man attacked you on the day of the race, stole your necklaces, and finished only the last little bit. Is that true?"

Caladur looked down at the two men. Yost was struggling to breath in some oxygen while Rundor had one of his massive arms around Yost's neck. As soon as the race was mentioned, Yost's eyes shot wide open in horror. He knew he'd been found out.

"Yes. He assaulted me on that day."

The champion squeezed a bit harder as Yost struggled to breath. "I've also heard that he had taken part in the kidnapping of a family. Is that true?"

"Yes."

The grasp tightened again. "Is there anything else you are aware of?"

"He rigged the semi-finals so he would choose the boars, he poisoned one of the participants so he would win the obstacle course, and he killed a man to steal his horse to have transportation to Lake Oznet."

Rundor looked down to the man he held in submission. "You have one chance to answer for these transgressions, and you'd better choose your response wisely. Are these true? Did you commit these acts?" Rundor dropped the man to the ground.

Yost gasped for air as soon as the champions hold was relinquished. The man laid on the dirt floor of the arena and looked up towards Caladur on the seating. "You're forgetting that I spit in his face just before," he screamed the rest at the top of his lungs, "I beat him in the finals!" The man tried to rise back to his feet before the end of a quarterstaff was planted in the middle of his chest, pinning him back down to the ground.

"Caladur Vandel," Rundor focused on the young elf in the stands above him, "it pleases me greatly invite you to be my apprentice."

The elf couldn't believe it. He thought that ship had sailed. He realized that he was wrong and he smiled.

"Tell him you accept," the old woman urged as she gently elbowed the elf's side.

"Yeah. I accept." Caladur grinned with joy. His journey had come to an end. He'd secured his position within the Fatiilian Arena.

"Good. Well, I must dispose of this garbage. Is there anything you'd like to say before I get rid of him?"

Yost spoke before Caladur could. "I've got money. I can," the rest of his air left him as the quarterstaff hit him in the chest causing him to roll around in an attempt to catch his breath yet again.

"He'll have money," Rundor told the breathless man.

"There's nothing I have to say to him."

"Good. Then meet me here in a week. You go rest and don't worry about anything. If you come see the page boy tomorrow morning, he'll have your first advance waiting for you. Great work Caladur. And I'll see you in a week."

"Thank you Rundor," he turned towards the elderly lady, "and thank you, for everything."

Caladur left the arena and made his way to *Sutur's This's and That's* to share the news and tidy up the store.

-40-

Six months had passed since Caladur became Rundor's apprentice. Throughout the experience, he had learned a good deal about life in general. Rundor became a sort of father to Caladur, something he never really had. The arena had just reopened now that the winter's ice had melted. Caladur now performed at an entirely new level. His physically developed body was comparable to those of the other champions after months of intense training.

In spite of the intensity of his training, Caladur managed to keep up his work at *Sutur's This's and That's*. He no longer required the income, but Mr. Sutur continued to insist on paying at least a token wage for the work the elf completed in the early mornings. Mr. Sutur's business was booming. He had opened up another store across the city and found the perfect manager for the shop. Tald.

Caladur entered *Tald's This's and That's* about an hour before the sun was to set. The outside of the shop looked identical to Mr. Sutur's. The only difference was the name that appeared on the outside. Lara had volunteered to paint the outside of the shop and again did a great job. When the storefront art had been completed, Mr. Sutur knew beyond the shadow of a doubt that she had been the one who painted his shop. The man made sure to compensate her for both paintings, but he still played as though he had no idea who had painted his beloved storefront.

The inside of the shop was furnished in a way that also matched Mr. Sutur's shop. Although the merchandise was a little different and catered towards Tald's personal tastes, the layout was identical. Once in the store, Caladur was greeted by a hearty welcome from Tald, his best friend. He had come to be the person that Caladur always hoped Oranton to become one day. A person he could rely on with his entire life and Tald knew he could do the same with Caladur.

"All set?"

"Yeah. Just picking up you and Lara on the way. You ready?"

"Just one minute." Tald finished arranging a few pieces of his merchandise. "Alright. Let's go see it." The pair of friends left and locked the store. The early spring brought with it cool air and pleasantly empty streets within Fatiil. Many people kept inside their warm homes if at all possible. The pair made their way to the housing district north of the arena where they picked up Lara from her home.

Caladur knocked gently on the door of Lara's home. She arrived in an instant.

"Ready?"

"Just a sec," Lara's voice called from inside the home.

Caladur heard frantic footsteps run around the inside of the home before she finally opened the door.

"Yup. My parents are already there, helping with a couple things I guess." She held a large rectangular object wrapped in brown paper in her arms.

"Alright. May I?" Caladur offered to carry the gift.

Lara accepted.

The trio walked through the city together. Every so often, Caladur and Lara would gaze into each other's eyes like the twitter pated young folks of Fatiil would often do. On the way to their destination, they passed through the arena district. The couple walked right passed Oranton and Aervaiel. The two elves appeared to be bickering with one another about some senseless problem they had run into. Caladur laughed to himself as he thought about the life he used to live.

As they continued on their way through the streets, Caladur's mind drifted to his mother. He hadn't heard from her since the day he ultimately renounced the Royal Order of True Elves. He was alright with that. Estine had become a sort of a mother for Caladur. She would not ever even think about betraying his trust. Or selling him out, like his natural mother had.

Caladur and Lara finally arrived at their destination. The home was two stories, and furnished for the most part, both on the inside and out with comfortable furniture, well-crafted tables, and art that was well-made. The young elf approached the door, didn't bother knocking and went inside.

"We're here," he called, but the discussion amongst friends muted the elf's words.

Within the home was everyone Caladur had come to love. Rundor, the champion of the Fatiilian Arena who took Caladur as his apprentice. Mr. Sutur, the man who gave Caladur the start he needed in order to survive inside the city. Tald's family. Uncle G and his wife were also in attendance, the family who happily accepted Caladur for who he was, even after he became romantically involved with their only daughter. Finally, but certainly not the least, Estine, Lucas and Celeste were within the home, after all, it was their home. The home they shared with Caladur who bought it with that intended purpose. Estine's family gave the homeless elf a shelter, a family and a community for him to rely on throughout his struggles. Now he had given them a home. The only person who was missing from the reunion was Owsin. He had taken his family with him to a small town which sat a few days to the west of Fatiil to be with his mother as she struggled with her health.

The scent of cooking food filled the home as the group of friends conversed with one another.

"Well. Aren't you going to open it?" Lara asked Caladur as she put the gift in front of him.

"Now?" he asked, "with everyone here?"

"Of course. They'll see it sooner or later. Why not sooner? Open it." She pushed the large package towards the elf.

Caladur set it down on the table and tore through the brown paper. He could tell by holding it that it was a painting and he thought he had a good idea of the subject. When the champion removed the wrapping, his suspicions were confirmed.

The depiction was of Caladur in his official arena attire. The elf was clothed in a tunic bearing his mark which was a hybrid of Rundor's crest and Estine's crest, the family he was now a part of, officially or not. His ensemble was primarily green with accents of blue, red, and purple on the trim. In his right hand, he held a metallic quarterstaff with sharpened points on either end, his preferred weapon. In the picture, he had his left food set upon a bull which strongly resembled the first beast the champion had slain within the arena.

Every inch of the painting was created with extreme care. It took most of the past month to create the work. Lara struggled with painting the gift in secrecy. She didn't have Caladur pose and composed the art from memory. She completed the art a week prior and had finally found the perfect oak frame to finish the piece the day before the dinner.

Caladur loved the painting. He gave the artist a gentle kiss and then hung the work above the fireplace for everyone to see. The painting remained on that wall until many years later when the home burnt down. It was the one object he had time to save from the home before the rest of his possessions were destroyed in the blaze.

The large group of people crammed their stomachs full of delicious food prepared by Estine and her sister for the housewarming party. The attendees shared stories of their lives, particularly ones that dealt with the journey of a young elf who was outcast from everything he knew, only to become a member of the Fatiilian arena.

But Caladur knew that the people were being too kind in paying homage to his journey. He knew that without the help of each and every person, no matter what type of blood rushed through their veins, he would not have been able to overcome the obstacles and struggles that stood before him on his journey to achieve his rightful place as Rundor's apprentice.

Made in the USA
Charleston, SC
16 January 2012